Ordinary Terrors

KITCHEN WITCH

Prologue

The first time Kevin Miller saw the dragon lady he was alone. The copse of trees was green and cool in the summer heat but that's not why he was there. There on a dare, the new kid on the block was being hazed by the boys in the hood. He knew it had to be a joke when they told him about the woman, make that the witch, who called dragons from the sky.

He waited for almost an hour before he heard her footsteps on the trail. Mrs. McGinn, "the dragon lady," had arrived. He scrunched himself behind a rotted log when he saw her. All he could hear now was the thud of his heart against his rib cage. He took a good look at her and nearly laughed out loud. What a colossal let down. She didn't look any different than any other woman he'd seen. She was about the same age as his mom. No costumes, amulets, black cat or broomstick. She could have been his mother for God's sake, except for that great mass of fiery red hair. He'd been had, time to ease out of his hiding place and find the other boys. He figured the whole neighborhood would be laughing at him by the time he got out of the woods. For now the day had become as silent as a tomb.

Then the sound came like a soft hum from far away. He paused, straining his ears to see if he could figure out where it was coming from. Might be one of those ultra light planes that would soon fly over them. But as the sound grew closer and more distinct, he knew it was no man made thing approaching.

Overhead a shadow blocked the light and warmth of the sun. Instinctively he shut his eyes and raised his arms over his head to protect his face. It could be birds, or worse yet, a swarm of bees. The shadow moved away from him. There was still a sound he couldn't identify, but it was not so loud now. He peeked through his fingers.

She stood only ten yards from him arms outstretched as though she was set to dive into a pool. Her face was so terrifyingly beautiful that he thought she didn't look real. She was smiling. The effect was hypnotizing. He found himself smiling too. He couldn't look away from her. He was happy, like Christmas morning happy, didn't know why, and didn't care either. He could stay here for hours just watching the lady with the red hair.

Suddenly it hit him with jaw dropping clarity that the lady was not alone. Though her face was naked the rest of her body was a teeming mass of fluttering insects. Of course he recognized what they were immediately and understood the reason why the boys called her the "dragon lady".

He figured the dragon flies had to number in the thousands. The thought struck him that all those insects must tickle her bare arms. But she didn't move a muscle the whole time they were there. Why did they come and how did she call them. This was some pretty heavy stuff for an eight year old. He watched a tear trickle down her cheek. Alarmed that the dragonflies might be biting her, he almost slid out of his hiding place but her face was calm, she was in no distress. It took only seconds for the dragon flies to lift as one and disappeared into the trees. A long sigh, and then she was gone too, back the way she had come.

Kevin wasn't sure how long he stayed behind that log. It must have been a long time because he was stiff and sore when he finally crawled out. At the edge of the trees five boys all about the same age waited for him. None of them spoke as they returned to their homes. They all knew what he'd seen.

Though no one mentioned it, somehow Kevin knew that none of them would talk about today, just as they never talked about their day with the dragon lady. The encounter was an unspoken rite of passage for the boys. The experience had changed each one of them, perhaps in different ways, but they sensed the distinction from pre-dragon lady and post dragon lady.

As the years passed, Kevin witnessed the dragon fly phenomenon several times. His initial feeling of unease passed quickly and with reason. The dragon lady had a daughter. On one of her excursions into the copse of trees, Kevin happened to come out of the grove a little sooner than he planned, and there she was, waiting on the path for her mom. Her face lit the afternoon when she smiled.

From that moment on, he knew that he would never want another thing in this world as badly as he wanted Janie. Janie McGinn was her name, and her flaming red hair, like her mothers', bore witness to her Irish descent. She was like all of his favorite things rolled into one glorious little body. She was sunshine on his face, hot fudge on his ice cream sundae; she was the lovely comfort of puppy breath, the softness of a freshly laundered sheet.

Janie, Janie, Janie. She was the first thing he thought about in the morning and the last thing he thought about before he fell asleep at night. When school started he and his buddies climbed into the school bus, pushing and shoving and acting like nine and ten year old ding bats always do on the first day. When he stopped short in the aisle, the other boys banged into him. She was sitting in the third seat from the front. His heart did a strange little fluttery thing as the boys behind him started pushing him forward.

His face was suddenly so hot he knew it had to be as red as a tomato. He finally found that his feet still worked and stumbled up the aisle. He took the seat behind her and hoped silently that she would turn around and speak to him. He also hoped she wouldn't. What could he possibly say to this amazing creature?

Tom Brookfield, Kevin's best friend, was the first one to pick up on the reason for his stranger than normal behavior and the game was on. All the way to school they badgered him about his "girlfriend". The only way he could get more uncomfortable was to have his pants fall down. Through all the jeering and guffaws,

Janie didn't turn around once, but if the boys could have seen her face they would have seen her smiling.

Janie took a little longer to warm up to Kevin. Exactly three days longer. On the bus, in the halls at school, the same scenario played out. Kevin was so smitten with her that he lost his ability to walk and talk. But on the third day of school something happened to change all that. Two boys in the class above Janie's ran smack into her in the hall. They knocked the books out of her arms and the wind out of her. Instead of picking up her books or apologizing, they just stood there and laughed like hyenas.

She struggled not to cry. She was about to pick up her books when a flash of denim and plaid shot by her, bumping the two older boys. Janie froze. Kevin stood in front of the two boys with a thunderous expression on his face. There was little doubt in their minds that he was furious. Kevin was tall for his age and well muscled from all the football he and his friends played. He held his ground, daring one of them to move in his or her direction. They didn't apologize to Janie or pick up her books but they did give her a sheepish look as they moved on down the hall. Without a word, Kevin picked up her books and gave them to her.

She felt like a princess rescued from an evil knight. When she finally spoke, she croaked out a thank you and lit his world with a smile.   From then on he had her heart. Kevin Miller and Janie McGinn were a twosome. They shared everything about themselves with each other. There wasn't a whole lot of history to recount; after all they were only nine years old. About the only things they never talked about were her mom's visits to the woods or the dragon flies.

Kevin wasn't the only new kid on the block that year. Two doors down from his house, and right next door to Tom's house, was the eyesore of the neighborhood. The house was a fixer upper to say the least. The asphalt siding was coming off in chunks, the roof was sway backed and the porch was rotting off. The grass hadn't been mowed all that spring. No one had lived there in several years according to the other boys. They thought it might be haunted. Sure looked like it could be.

About half way through the school year the house began to change. No one could say for sure whether a crew had come in on weekdays when everyone else in the neighborhood was at work or in school, or if someone was doing repairs at night. The house grew new vinyl siding, sprouted new windows and a new front door. Once in a while a neighbor would comment on the transformation, but no one was curious enough to wonder about it very much. No one that is except Jamie's mom. She often paused in front of the house on her walks, cocking her head as if she were waiting or listening for something.

One morning a little girl no one had seen before waited at the bus stop. She was the first one there as the bus stop was in front of her house. Her house was the one with odd looking windows and front door, the one that had somehow been transformed while no one was looking. The shape and placement of the dark windows gave the impression that they were brooding eyes that stared out at the neighborhood. The overly large front door was a garish red, with tiny dark windows trimmed in white. One could almost imagine that it was a gaping mouth. The renovation did nothing to improve the feeling of unease it gave people.

The new owners must have moved in during the nighttime hours. No one had seen a moving van or the rest of the family, just this little girl.

Kevin glanced at Tom, a comment dying on his lips. Tom looked like he'd been hit in the stomach. Kevin didn't say anything. He turned his attention to the girl who definitely had all of Tom's at the moment. Her hair was long and black as night, hanging kind of haphazardly down to her waist. She looked up and saw him staring at her. Something about her eyes wasn't right. They were too dark, somehow cold.

Her eyes evidently didn't bother Tom. He was grinning like an idiot. By lunch time Tom knew all about her. Her name was Laura LaQua. Her family moved here from New Orleans, and she was in his history class. Kevin didn't say much to Tom about Laura. He didn't want to put a chink in their friendship, but he didn't really care much for her. She was pushy and bossy but worse than that, he had a feeling that she didn't like Janie. There was nothing he could put his finger on. Laura went out of her way to let everyone know that Janie was her BFF. Laura's other friends, which were few, were an odd faction of trouble makers and misfits.

Laura seemed to have the same affect on his other friends. They tended to drift away when she was around. The LaQua family kept to themselves and was rarely seen. They were never present for block parties or fund raisers. Curiously, no one seemed to mind that all invitations went unanswered. Tom had few friends left by the time they all graduated from High School, but he still had Kevin and Janie and of course his Laura.

Kevin and Tom always planned to go to Michigan State University together. Both were accepted there, Kevin majoring in Law and Tom in Veterinary medicine.

Janie chose to attend the University of Michigan, majoring in psychology. She planned to be a counselor to troubled teens. The psychology program there was excellent and U of M wasn't that far from MSU, so she could come home often. Their parents were all delighted with their choice of schools.

Kevin came to love and respect Jenny McGinn over the years. She was a kind and loving soul, always smiling and willing to help out in the community in whatever capacity she could. She was very well liked in the neighborhood and fun to be with. She adored Kevin and that was good enough for him. So the lady liked dragon flies, and they liked her. Everyone had some sort of idiosyncrasy.

Laura didn't go to college as such. She spent her time studying with a special group of educators dealing in the paranormal. Knowing Laura as they did no one was surprised. Where and when she attended these classes was a mystery in itself. She hardly ever left her house although she seemed to have frequent late night visitors. It didn't matter much anyway; everyone was so busy with classes and homework that they hardly had time to think about her choice of academia.

College was a new kind of grind. The first year Kevin and Tom spent ninety nine percent of their time either going to class or studying for the next one. Two things made it all bearable; the infrequent weekend trips home and the fact that the two guys were together. Even more, Tom was another person away from home, and Laura. He was more like his old self. On weekends he would report in to Laura and hardly anyone would see him till Sunday night when it was time to go back to school.

Janie excelled in school. The only drawback was of course, missing Kevin. On weekends she and Kevin and all their old friends would get together and party, compare college stories and catch up with the latest news.

Tom and Laura seldom attended these get-togethers but when they did it sort of put a damper on everyone's good humor. Janie began to realize that she felt better, lighter and more confident when Laura wasn't around.

By the time Kevin was in his senior year he was being interviewed by some pretty impressive law firms. Two months before graduation he was hired by a very prestigious firm in Lansing Michigan. It seemed there was really nothing to keep him and Janie from getting married now. She already had her degree and several interviews coming up. He'd purchased the ring, a perfect two carat blue diamond from Yanks, his hometown jeweler. He'd picked it out two years ago.

He planned a beautiful weekend for them. Dinner and dancing at a swank supper club and a carefully orchestrated proposal, with a little help from some friends who played musical instruments, including Tom. While they were eating dessert, the guys would surround them playing her favorite song," Lost in Your Eyes". The waiter would then appear with a bottle of champagne on a tray with the open ring box next to the glasses. With all that going on he would then drop to one knee and ask her to be his wife. How could she say no? Perfect.

Funny how the best plans in the world can't stop an imperfect reality. The weekend was three days away when the phone call came. Janie's mom was extremely ill. Janie was already at her mother's side in the hospital.

Kevin immediately canceled his plans and drove home to be with them. Two days later, she slipped in to a coma and quietly passed away. Janie, who had been a rock until then, was now inconsolable. Her mother was her only family. Now there was no one left. Who could she talk to? Her mother was her confidant and her mentor. Her grief was overwhelming.

Kevin stepped in to do what Kevin did best. He took charge, making all the funeral arrangements with respect to the requests Mrs. McGinn had made to Janie before she passed. Unlike most funerals, hers would be held entirely out of doors. She asked that the ceremony be brief and kept small. Of course that proved to be impossible as the whole town turned out to pay their respects. A family friend from out of town sang two hymns that were her favorite. Her voice was as pure as the sky was blue that day.

A cleansing peace filled the silence. The breeze rustling through the trees was the only sound. Janie smiled at Kevin and squeezed his hand. It was time to move on. Life would never be the same without her, but life would go on just the same. There was still much to do before they could get back to any kind of a routine. There was the estate to settle and decisions to be made about the house. But for the moment all they wanted to do was to savor this tiny slice of time. The entire world stood still, focusing on this gathering of those who knew this remarkable woman, and then the thing that they had never talked about, hadn't even hinted at, was suddenly right in front of them and everyone there.

Thousands of wings beat a sound like nothing anyone had ever heard. No one moved as the amazing cloud of dragonflies descended to the casket. Softly, ever so softly the mass settled there and was still. The breeze had ceased. The moment seemed timeless as their presence filled the elements. One might expect surprise at such a phenomenon, there was none. It was as though the winged visitors were expected. Those who were present that day couldn't be sure if they had taken a breath for those moments. As one the shimmering mass rose above the gravesite, hovering in a perfect circle before slowly rising into the sky and out of sight.

If a sense of understanding could be put into words, they might have said that the soul of Jenny McGinn was ushered to paradise on the gossamer wings of creatures that looked a lot like dragonflies. Later, as the ceremony broke up, comments would be heard such as, "wasn't it a remarkable and beautiful coincidence that the flowers on the casket attracted such an amazing swarm" and, "It seemed like nature stepped in to bless her passing," and "what kind of butterflies were they?"

The LaQua family was characteristically not present but sent a curious conglomeration of flowers with an odd scent. The card simply read, "We feel the loss of her presence," and signed it, "The LaQua family."

When Kevin read it he thought it an odd remark as they could hardly have known her. Janie said nothing, sliding it into the envelope that held the cards she would later send thank you notes for.

Mrs. McGinn's will was short and sweet, leaving a generous bequest of money to local charities and all else to her beloved daughter Janie. The only shocker was the sum total of her assets. It was true that the McGinns were never in want for anything, even though Mr. McGinn had passed on shortly after Janie's birth, but Janie had no idea how wealthy they were. Money was never a subject they discussed. Finding herself an heiress, Janie had a hard time equating the modest lifestyle she had always known to the considerable fortune she now found herself in possession of.

Kevin thought it best to give Janie a few days to sort out her mother's personal things and to deal with her grief in her own way. She was grateful that he understood her needs. In a few days she wished to heaven that others were as understanding.

Laura breezed in to the house unannounced two days later. She spewed out her profound sorrow for Janie's loss but seemed infinitely more interested in helping her go through her mother's personal belongings than comforting a friend. There did seem to be a lot of correspondence in her mother's desk. Some of the people and places Janie did not recognize. Laura had most of them in her hand with an eye toward sorting through them when an odd feeling crept over Janie. She laid a hand on Laura's arm.

"This is a task I prefer to handle on my own Laura." She softened it with, "I do appreciate the offer though."

For just a millisecond a veil fell over Laura's eyes. Something cold and menacing there. She blinked and it was gone. Janie's emotional state had her imagination flying off in all sorts of strange directions. She needed to keep herself grounded and focused. There was a great deal to do before she could resume her life. She put her grief on the back burner to work her way through all of this. Not the wisest choice, but her experience with loss was almost nonexistent. Her father died before she was old enough to remember him and her grandparents died in the wake of a terrible earth quake while visiting the orient before she was born.

The only other death in her life that she could remember was a very old, very fat gold fish that she accidentally overfed. The toilet bowl burial had been brief.

Laura was not to be put off, offering to help her sort through other things instead. Janie saw no problem with that. She put Laura in the master bedroom to pack up her mother's cosmetics, curlers, combs, brushes, toothbrushes etc. in plastic bags. These things would be discarded. With Laura in the other room she turned her attention to her mother's desk. Now that she thought about it, she remembered many nights that her mother had stayed up late writing letters and making notes in her diary. Her Diary!! Where was it? Ignoring everything else, she began pulling open drawers, looking for the leather bound ledger that her mother spent so much time on.

The bottom drawer was locked. She rattled and pulled and yanked, putting a foot to the desktop for leverage, all to no avail. "Please open, "she pleaded, and found herself on her rear end a few feet from the desk. The drawer had sprung open and was lying in her lap. Right on top was the leather diary. The moment she touched it she began to sob. Anguish poured out in torrents. She may have been that way for hours or minutes, she didn't know. She felt emptiness deeper than anything she had ever known. The leather diary was clasped to her breast.

Her fingers traced the beautifully embossed dragonfly on its cover. "Mom", she whispered. Her mother's presence touched her, reaching out to sooth her. Somehow she knew she would never lose this ability to bask in her mother's nearness.

Suddenly chilled, another presence cast a shadow over the moment. Laura stood in the doorway staring. The toiletries she held forgotten, her gaze was locked on to the leather journal in Janie's grasp. An awkward silence hung between them.

Janie found her voice, formed a smile, "Thank you for your help Laura, but I think I need some time alone to deal with all this, you understand."

Laura seemed not to hear her. Still locked on to the diary she took a few steps closer. Her eyes looked as though she had been hypnotized.

"Laura, I think I need some time alone, o.k.?"

The blank stare was blinked away. She took a deep breath as if she'd been holding it for a long time. She allowed herself to be ushered to the door. She stood on the other side for some time. She would find a way.

It would be three weeks before anyone would see Janie though she kept in touch with Kevin by phone. He couldn't imagine surviving the loss of his own mother and was very patient, allowing Janie all the time she needed.

Emerging from her grief and self imposed solitude, Janie was ready to pick up the pieces of her life. Her outgoing personality and sweet demeanor seemed bubblier than ever. Kevin was so relieved he couldn't seem to wipe the dopey smile off his face.

He asked casually about her mother's house and belongings. Janie gave him a non-committal answer, something to the effect that it was a work in progress. He was happy to settle for that.

The following Saturday night, they ate their dinner in their very favorite restaurant. They were so comfortable it seemed hard to believe that only a month had passed since her mother had passed away. They had a wonderful dinner, though neither of them could have remembered what they ate. They were too intent on each other. Janie, always beautiful, had a special glow about her tonight. Couples passing couldn't help smiling at them. The moment was right.

Kevin dropped his fork, (a prearranged signal), and suddenly they were surrounded by four young men, guitars in hand singing their rendition of "Lost in Your Eyes." Janie was used to these characters pranking each other, laughing and clapping her hands she hardly noticed the tray the waiter set on the table. Everyone in the restaurant was enjoying themselves.

Kevin watched her face as her gaze fell on the tray. Champagne, two glasses, and an open ring box graced the charger. Her breath caught as he dropped to one knee. The entire restaurant was suddenly bathed in silence as he took her hand.

He hardly had a chance to finish asking when she threw her arms around his neck shouting, "Yes, yes, yes!"

The place exploded, everyone clapping, ladies daubed at their eyes with hankies, couples embraced.

It had an air of family. It couldn't have been more perfect. Tom's eyes were misty as he shook his best friend's hand. People stopped at their table to congratulate them as they left the restaurant. Friends began to trickle in to join the celebration, ordering more champagne, everyone talking at once. It was glorious.

Janie's best friend, Cindy, hugged her hard enough to squeeze the breath out of her. Everyone wanted to know where and how soon. Those things hadn't been decided yet so the talk abruptly turned to bachelor and bachelorette parties. In just a few minutes it was decided that they would combine the two and invite everybody. More laughter, more toasts, more ideas. Everyone was here to wish them well. The love and friendship shared by all of them was infectious.

In all the excitement, Kevin realized he'd lost track of Tom. When he saw him coming through the door his smile wavered just a bit. Of course he'd gone to get Laura. The temperature in the room dropped ten degrees. Laura raced across the room screeching like a banshee, but instead of grabbing Janie, she latched on to Kevin, arms locked around his neck and lips locked on his mouth. The silence was palpable. No one moved.

Laura pushed herself away laughing and joking that it was all in good fun. Uncomfortable onlookers laughed nervously, shuffling feet and clearing throats. Kevin was dumbfounded. He couldn't think of anything to say. He gave Janie a sheepish look, not knowing what to expect. Relief washed over him. All he saw in her beautiful eyes was amusement. He kissed her tenderly, congratulating himself again that such a woman was truly his. An audible sigh of relief filled the room.

The only person who seemed unhappy was Laura. She sulked the remainder of the evening. It was safe to assume that every soul in the room pitied poor Tom his choice of a female companion. On the way home Kevin tried to apologize for Tom's girlfriend's actions but Janie laid a finger across his lips.

"Laura is not something you have to worry about Kevin. I know what she is." An odd comment, he thought. The way she'd said *something* instead of someone and *what* instead of who.

She snuggled close while he drove, his tension passing with the miles. He was so proud of her, so much in love with her. Nothing could ever change what they had together. But *something* was about to test that certainty in ways that he never could have imagined.

Life returned to normal then. Some went back to school; others were looking for or starting new jobs. Kevin was the latest addition to the firm of Craig, Philbrecht, and Carol. He was junior man on the totem to be sure, but was garnering respect from his colleagues with his instincts and abilities. More and more clients were being diverted to his office. The cases grew more complex as the months flew by. He truly loved what he was doing. As a prosecutor he felt he could make a difference in the community. Every bad guy he helped put away meant one less threat to the city and people he loved.

Janie was still in the interview phase of her career. She wanted to be sure she had the right niche. Money was never going to be a problem for them, so she could take her time deciding what she wanted to do and where.

Tom still had two more grueling years before he could put the letters D.V.M. after his name. He loathed having to be away from all his friends during the week and tried to get home as many weekends as he could in spite of his hectic schedule. Still he enjoyed what he was doing. He loved animals and being able to make them well was the most rewarding thing he had ever done.

This weekend he had to get home. Kevin and Janie's bachelor/bachelorette party was Saturday night. He had to juggle a few things but cleared Saturday and Sunday to go home for the festivities. He and some of the other guys had a few surprises for the party planned. Driving home his thoughts turned to Laura. A feeling of unease seeped into his thoughts. Her behavior the night of the engagement had been tasteless to say the least. They fought about it all the way home that night. He still didn't know how she had cajoled him out of his anger. He found himself at his apartment, in his bed, with her on top of him and no recollection of how he got there.

It didn't matter after that. All he could think of, all he could taste, smell and feel was Laura. She was his world. When he wasn't with her he yearned for her so intensely it hurt to breathe. Still there were times when thinking about her brought on this same uneasiness.

This particular night on his way home he thought again of how she held him spellbound. When he took time to think about her now, he realized that she was not really beautiful in the classic sense. She possessed no special talents or skills that he was aware of, except of course in bed. He knew deep down that none of his friends liked her. Hell his own parents didn't like her. They never said so, but they didn't have to. He could tell.

She seemed to bring out the worst in everyone but him. Why he loved her above all else he couldn't say. He only knew he did. Sometimes he found himself wondering why he was more self assured and more comfortable when he was some distance from her.

As the miles lessened, his peace of mind did the same. The closer he got to home, the more he felt her pulling at him. The desire to see her was like a fast moving cancer. By the time he hit the city limits he was desperate to get to her.   Thoughts of the party or anything else buried themselves somewhere in the depths of his mind. He was almost there now. Obsession grew stronger than logic. He was too caught up to feel the depth of his misery. He had to get back to his Laura.

Saturday night and the party was in full swing. Everyone was having a blast. Food, drink, story swapping about their misspent youths and tall tales that merely skimmed the truth, never quite escaping a healthy dash of bullshit filled the room. Even Laura couldn't seem to dampen anyone's spirits.

Tom and the rest of the guys pulled a few balloon condom tricks and produced a baby stroller built for triplets complete with three of the ugliest dolls they could find inside. They had name tags around their necks that read; Dumb, Dumber, and Dumbest. Everyone roared.

The hours flew by and people were just beginning to think it might be time to leave when Laura took the room.

"May I have everyone's attention please?" The room fell silent.

"As Janie's BFF I have decided to give her a very special bridal shower, and of course everyone here is invited." More silence.

"All we need from the bride and groom is a definite wedding date." She smiled. "How about it you two, when's the big day?"

Trapped like rats, Kevin thought. They hadn't firmed up a date yet. Janie only smiled up at him and answered sweetly, "June twenty third. I hope that gives you enough time to make your plans Laura."

"More than enough time Janie, more than enough."

Of course Laura knew none of Kevin or Janie's friends would decline the invitation to the bridal shower. They would put aside their dislike for Laura for the couple's sake.

No one was surprised that the shower would not be held at the LaQua mansion. They were relieved she reserved a banquet room at a local hotel. Neither did anyone find it strange that the self appointed BFF was not asked to be maid of honor or even a bridesmaid.

Kevin's mother and father insisted on helping with the wedding, not so much for the financial part of it, (Kevin had explained Janie's situation to them.) Mr. and Mrs. Miller felt they could lend support to Janie in other ways, Janie not having any parents now. Mrs. Miller stepped in and tried to do all she thought the mother of a bride should do, while Kevin's dad led him through groom's responsibilities.

Tom would of course be Kevin's best man. With just over a month before the wedding, all the girls were atwitter with bridesmaids' fittings and helping Janie with her dress, jewelry etc. The Millers hired the catering company and secured the country club for the reception. They also decided to give the kids two weeks in Hawaii for a wedding gift. The family's Pastor, father Bill, was delighted with Janie. They instantly became friends. She was so lovely and sweet it was easy to see why Kevin had fallen in love with her. There was also something about her, strength within her quite unlike anything he had ever encountered.

The bridal shower could have been a dismal affair but for Janie's sweet disposition and the obvious happiness she and Kevin shared. The food was a concoction of foreign tastes and textures no one could identify. Laura proclaimed that shower food was boring and she wanted to do something out of the ordinary. There was enough left over to feed half the population of the town. The games were another "Laura" adaptation.

Balloons were held between the guy's legs while the girls were to pry them loose and put them between their own legs by rubbing up against them with their thighs. Hands were to be kept behind their backs. Laura made an exhibition of herself getting her balloon from Tom, gyrating like a stripper.

The presents were many and wonderful. Some turned out to be pranks from some of Kevin's more imaginative friends which made for a fun time. Janie opened the last gift, a lovely cut crystal decanter and six wine glasses. She was thanking everyone for the wonderful gifts when Laura produced one more.

The box was wrapped in black crepe secured with a garish red ribbon. The moment she touched it Janie felt uncomfortable. The two women locked eyes. Laura's were crinkled with amusement.

"Well what are you waiting for girlfriend? Open it."

When she pulled on the ribbon the box sprung open of its own accord. Nestled in black tissue, unique in design and obviously expensive was a kitchen witch. She was ten inches tall with straw colored hair that looked almost real. Her dress was beautifully hand stitched and black as pitch. Her features were so realistically crafted one could almost see her chest rise and fall. But the most unusual thing about her was her eyes. A silver cord was attached to her back from which she would hang. When Janie held her up for all to see, no matter which way she spun her eyes seemed to follow Janie.

For just a heartbeat the spinning stopped her eyes boring into Janie's. She nearly dropped the witch. It felt like a bolt of electricity. For Janie time stood still. Nothing and no one remained in the void where they existed. As if in slow motion the witch began to spin again, the eyes nothing more than opaque orbs of colored glass. Laura's voice broke the spell.

"Isn't it just the most darling thing Janie? I found it in New Orleans in a terribly expensive, terribly exclusive little out of the way place just off Bourbon Street. The old woman who owned the place is touted to be a real live witch! Isn't that delicious?" Laughing she bent close to Janie's ear.

"I'm told that kitchen witches bring good luck to the home they are given to live in."

For the benefit of the others Laura explained that back in the sixties and seventies kitchen witches were all the rage. They were routinely given at house warming parties and bridal showers as a token of good luck. She hoped to renew the practice with her gift to Kevin and Laura.

The room was quiet. Everyone seemed to be waiting for Janie to say something. She cleared her throat and smiled at her guests, thanking Laura for the thoughtful gift. No one would have suspected the sudden hopelessness that overcame her for those few seconds.

The kitchen witch, along with the other gifts, was packed off to the house where the newlyweds would take up residence after the honeymoon. The bridesmaids and Mrs. Miller would ready the house while they were away. The beautiful Cape Cod style home was one of many perks Kevin would receive from Craig, Philbrecht and Carol in the coming years. The home was leased in Kevin's name with the option to purchase.

In the meantime, Janie stayed in her mother's house and Kevin stayed in his apartment. Decisions on the house and apartment would be made later on down the road. Kevin was sure he could sublet his apartment, but he wasn't sure what Janie would decide to do with her mom's place yet.

Time flew by. It was suddenly June with the wedding only a few days away.

A thousand details had to be seen to. Janie's choice of bridesmaids simplified each task. And now it was the wedding day.

It didn't seem possible that June twenty third had come so quickly. The bride was breathtakingly beautiful. The wedding, though short in duration was touching and perfectly fitting for the bride and groom.

As was expected the reception was filled with happiness, raucous laughter and well wishers. There was food and drink aplenty, enough to sate every appetite. Toast after toast was made. Neither Kevin nor Janie had time to eat a bite between glasses clinking for them to kiss yet again. They didn't seem to mind.

As soon as reasonably possible, the bride and groom made their exit to the bridal suite. Their plane left for Hawaii at seven the next morning.

For the next fourteen days they thought of nothing but each other. The weather was beautiful; the air fragrant with tropical flowers, and the ocean was exquisitely blue and welcoming. They swam, sunbathed, ate like little pigs, and made love until they were exhausted. A perfect beginning for a perfect life.

Back from the honeymoon, Kevin made a huge fuss about carrying his bride over the threshold of their new home. They giggled their way into the foyer. He held her close, nuzzling her neck. She smiled into the rooms that were theirs together. The girls had done a fantastic job. The house was spotless. Everything had been put away for them. The house welcomed them home.

Suddenly she stiffened in his arms. He followed her gaze to the stemware cabinet above the island. Suspended from it spun the kitchen witch on her silver cord. The shadow she cast on the counter seemed much too large and dark for the tiny figure. She shivered as he put her on her feet. He felt like he was caught between the rock and the hard place.

"Look Janie, I know you hate that damned thing, I'm not too fond of it myself, but Tom is my best friend. Can we wait just long enough for them to see it hanging there before we chuck it in the trash?"

Janie was relieved that he understood how she felt. She had to give a little too.

"You're right; I know Tom would be hurt if we didn't hang the disgusting thing in our kitchen." Then in her best imitation of Laura she added, "After all it is a kitchen witch and it's supposed to be good luck dar'lin."

Kevin picked her up and swung her around. How in this world did he ever get lucky enough to end up with this stunning creature?

The witch spun faster on her silver cord, she was home at last.

Life resumed. Kevin went back to his law firm; Janie began the tedious search for just the right position. She was in no hurry. Settling into married life took some getting used to but she found herself adapting very well to being the keeper of the hearth and home. She enjoyed having a nice dinner ready when Kevin got home. She and her girlfriends shopped for weeks to complete the furnishings for all the rooms. Kevin chuckled and nodded his approval each time he came home to find that something had been added.

When the last rug was laid, the last curtain hung and the final chair was placed, Janie sat for a long while just looking around at their home. It was part Janie, with the wall hangings area rugs, sheer curtains with antique tie backs and part Kevin with the overstuffed easy chair, the massive recliner, family pictures, and his favorite, ugly to be sure, reading lamp from his apartment.

Perfect. "Welcome home Mr. & Mrs. Kevin Miller." She sighed.

Movement drew her attention to the kitchen. Spinning like an out of control top, the kitchen Witch was almost a blur. Janie glanced at the windows to see if any were left open to the breeze blowing outside. They were all closed.

Hairs on the back of her neck tingled as she approached the tiny dervish. Instinct told her to back away. Common sense told her to touch it. Inches from the whirling figure she froze. The violent spinning stopped. The witch stared at her, eyes filled with loathing. Her mind clicked. She knew those eyes.

"Who are you?" She whispered. "What are you?"

Laura's eyes crinkled with amusement. Her mind clicked again. Of course it was Laura. It had always been Laura.

She wanted to grab the little menace by its throat but the thought of touching it was so repugnant to her she felt sick. The witch began to spin.

She retreated to the sofa.

"Mom, I need you. I've never needed you so much. I'm afraid I'm losing my mind. You would know what to do. If only you could talk to me like you used to." Her head in her hands she sobbed. "Please mom, I feel so helpless. Why did you leave me?" she cried.

Soft as a sigh, a flutter, like the wing of a butterfly, gently flitted across her cheek. Boneless, she fell easily into a peaceful sleep; a sweet smile graced her face as the menace was held at bay.

Kevin found her like that when he got home. He kissed her forehead, deciding to let her sleep. She was so beautiful it nearly took his breath away just to look at her. After eating a sandwich and reading the paper he checked on her once more. She was still sleeping soundly. "You must have had quite a day my love," He sighed. His lips brushed hers as he whispered good night.

The tranquil scene in the living room did not go unnoticed. The witch shook with agitation. Eyes burning, she took in the serenity of their devotion. Her eyes filled with yearning as they followed him out of the room.

Her attention snapped back to the sleeping woman on the sofa. She controlled the urge to cackle out loud. In a short time, all that she and her kind had plotted and schemed for would be won. The old powers could not stop her now. Her nemesis was no longer alive.

Convinced that the powers she feared were also dead, she assured herself that nothing or no one could stop her now.

Janie woke refreshed with no recollection of the encounter with the witch in the kitchen. She must have fallen asleep after her shopping spree with the girls yesterday. She hadn't even heard Kevin come home last night. She busied herself with making a breakfast of bacon, hash browns and silver dollar pancakes. She poured a hot cup of coffee and tip toed in to wake him. She hadn't given the witch a second glance as she worked in the kitchen that morning.

Oblivious to the anger emanating from the hovering observer above them, they enjoyed their morning together. Awash with fresh rage it pondered anew the ability of the woman to recover herself so quickly. It was time for a summoning. A summoning would tip the scales in her favor. At once the horror occupying the dangling figure was gone, leaving only a nicely crafted and quite useless piece of tchotchke.

Four wonderful months passed without incident. The Millers had settled into a comfortable routine. Friends called from time to time, always phoning first in case the honeymooners were still honeymooning. They enjoyed welcoming them to their home. Everyone brought either a bottle of wine or a small house warming gift of some sort.

On one such occasion, Janie's college roommate, Katie, dropped by with a new boyfriend. He was an improvement over the last one. No shrapnel in his eyebrows or nose, no visible tattoos, and when he opened his mouth, he was polite and seemed to possess a modicum of intelligence. When the girls went to the kitchen to open yet another bottle of wine, Katie professed that he was *the one*. Something

Janie had heard many times in the past four years. Reaching for wine goblets, Katie's eyes fell on the witch overhead.

"Holy shit Janie, why in hell did you keep that ugly piece of crap? It gives me the creeps." She shuddered.

Janie laughed. "I can't throw the thing out in the trash till Tom and Laura see it hanging there at least once." She sighed.

Katie's brows shot up. "You mean the queen bitch hasn't been here yet? I didn't think she could stay away from Kevin that long."

Janie shot her a look. "I know she makes everyone feel uncomfortable Katie, but we have to remember that Tom is nuts about her, and Tom is a good friend."

"As to her crush on Kevin, well I'm not sure if any of that is true or not. She likes him, but I think she is just trying her best to be closer to me. I kind of feel sorry for her. She has no friends that I know of." She popped the cork. "Anyway, because of the guy's friendship I put up with her."

"O.K. girlfriend, don't say I didn't warn you. Now let's have some of that wine." She carried the tray of glasses while Janie carried the wine bucket.

The company was good, the talk at times hilarious, reminiscing about their college days and some of the quirky professors they shared. Still the night had soured for Janie. She didn't feel very well. After the guests left she turned in early, hoping to fend off the queasy stomach she'd developed about halfway through her glass of wine. Kevin offered to straighten up while she took a leisurely shower. Snuggled together in bed she assured him and herself that she would be all better in the morning. But when Kevin woke up it was three A.M. and Janie was in the bathroom getting rid of her dinner. He opened the door to a pale shaking Janie, sitting on the floor with her head over the toilet. "Sweetie, are you all right?" Two strides and he was holding her around the waist. She smiled up at him.

"I think the wine didn't agree with me. I also think I'm done. No more wine for awhile." She swore.

But she wasn't done. Convinced she had the flu, she made an appointment to see her family doctor. Sitting in the waiting room she began to feel foolish. Her stomach had settled down and she felt fine. She was almost to the point of telling the receptionist that she thought she would cancel, when Helen, his nurse called her name.

Helen was all smiles and congratulations as she put Janie on the scale, took her blood pressure and temperature.

"Well everything is normal so far kiddo. You've gained five pounds so I'm going to assume marriage agrees with you." She giggled. Then, boom she was out the door.

"Five pounds! If this keeps up I'll look like a blimp in no time with all this wedded bliss!" And then it hit her. She already knew what Dr. D was going to tell her after he examined her. She gasped. "Could it be, already?" They hadn't taken any precautions. Still it seemed impossibly soon.

The grin on Dr. D's face told her that her suspicions were correct.

"You and Kevin didn't waste any time did you?"

She was speechless. She left the doctor's office in a daze. A baby, their baby. She hadn't suspected. She knew Kevin didn't either. As she drove, something besides the baby began to grow inside her. The closer to home she got the greater and stronger it got. A new kind of happiness blossomed in her. A child, conceived from their love, a part of the two of them. Nothing on earth had ever given her this much joy. She drove a little faster. She couldn't wait to get home and prepare a special dinner and plan on just the perfect way to tell him.

"Milk for you from now on lady, and no more wine." She chided herself.

Dinner was perfect, as Kevin told her for the fifth time. Curled up together on the sofa, he could almost feel the excitement building in her.

"O.K. spill it. You've been dying to tell me something since I got home tonight. What is it?"

Just the right moment, was now! "We're pregnant!" she blurted.

Kevin almost dropped his wine glass. "Honest to God?"

His eyes welled up as she nodded. "Oh my sweet, perfect Janie, a baby! I can't believe it! I'm going to be a daddy! You're going to be a mommy!" He hooted loud enough for the neighbors to hear.

He pulled her closer, kissing her face, stroking her hair. Life couldn't be more complete. He thought he might burst with happiness. He let her go and started dialing everyone they knew, starting with his parents. They were squealing and crying into the phone. They asked if they could come over, and Kevin was delighted. "Of course you can. Come and celebrate with us. You're about to be grandparents!"

And come they did. Dad had a bottle of champagne, mom a bouquet of roses and a handkerchief to her eyes the entire evening. By the time the Millers turned in it was very late, but everyone they knew had heard the news, everyone that is but Tom and Laura. He didn't know why he hadn't called his best friend to give him the news. Every time he reached for the phone he put it off.

In the ensuing months they didn't see much of Tom and nothing of Laura. Janie was getting a very pronounced baby bump that Kevin could not keep his hands off. Either he was patting her belly or listening to it with his ear planted against her belly button.

With only a few weeks to go before Janie's due date, she happened to be out shopping for the perfect

mobile for the babies' room when she ran into Laura.
The look on Laura's face when she saw Janie's
protruding belly was unfathomable. She reached out a
hand toward Janie's belly, and to her shame, Janie
recoiled. She wasn't sure why, it was instinctive.
Laura gave her a knowing look and spouted her
congratulations.

"Oh you must let me give the most elaborate baby
shower Janie!" She spouted.

Janie felt her smile stiffen. She remembered the last
time Laura gave a party for her and Kevin.

The smile wavered on Laura's face when Janie told
her Cindy and Katie already had that handled and
assured Laura that she would get an invitation soon.
With that she made her excuses and fled the
department store.

The following evening Tom and Laura showed up unannounced. Tom carried a basket of baby bottles and pacifiers. Laura carried a large box with holes punched in the top and sides. Janie had just tidied up the kitchen and was looking forward to a quiet night, just the two of them. She was anything but pleased to see them.

Laura barged in, slamming the box on the counter top. She bear hugged Janie, and kissed Kevin on the cheek. Janie smiled a welcome and Kevin offered to give them a tour of the place. Laura grinned like a Cheshire cat at the spinning witch above her. "Oh I just knew she would be happy here", she gushed. "And didn't I tell you she would bring you luck?" Something in Laura's eyes made Janie's heart skip a beat. They snapped and crinkled at the corners. A familiar memory struggled to surface. Laura hurried to catch up with the guys who were heading down stairs.

Janie shook herself mentally. She could hear the cackle of Laura's laughter wafting up the stairs. "She sounds like an old witch." She whispered. She gasped as her world tilted. Above her the eyes of the devil doll came to life. Laura stared back at her. Her mind felt as if it were floating away from her. She reached for it. She held tight to the counter top, for the moment her only grasp on reality.

"I need to remember something. If I can just pull it forward. Concentrate Janie, find it again." She pleaded with her subconscious.

Then the box on the counter moved and all coherent thought left her.

She realized Kevin was speaking to her. "Shall I serve the wine downstairs or wait till they get done with their game of foosball and bring them back up here?"

She glanced at the open bottle and glasses on the tray in front of her. She didn't remember setting up the serving tray or opening the wine. When she didn't answer Kevin said, "I know this isn't what you wanted to do this evening but we may as well make the best of it now. By the way what's with the box?" He asked, giving it a poke.

Janie found her tongue. "I'm afraid I don't know, but I think it's alive." She whispered.

The laughter died on his lips as he realized she wasn't joking. He could see how pale she was.

 "You aren't feeling well are you?" He pushed at the box. Nothing happened. "Honey, what makes you think there's something alive in the box?" He poked at it again.

She didn't answer him, just kept staring at the cardboard box. This pregnancy was having an effect on her. He figured there would be mood swings, but he didn't know it would send her imagination into overdrive. She did look tired though, and a little frightened.

He picked up the tray.

"Tell you what, why don't you get comfortable in the living room while I take care of our guests? Just rest awhile. I'm sure they won't mind, and I don't think they'll stay very long at any rate."

"Maybe you're right Kev. I am a little tired. I'll just put my feet up for a few minutes. I'll be fine." When she turned toward the living room, Laura stood in the doorway.

"Hey where are you going girlfriend. You can't abandon us just yet. You haven't opened the gift we brought you. You're just going to die when you see it!" She was like an over inflated bubble ready to burst.

"Janie's just a little tired Laura." Kevin offered. "How about doing this some other night?"

Nonplussed Laura pushed the box across the counter. "Oh you just have to open this now Janie. You'll understand when you see what's inside. Then we'll call it an early evening. Here you go." She pushed the box closer still.

Tom was beginning to feel uncomfortable. Janie was obviously not feeling well. "Maybe we should do this another time Laura." He suggested.

He asked himself for the tenth time why the hell he'd let her talk him into barging in on them tonight. He was also having second thoughts about her choice of gifts.

Laura shot him a murderous look. "No Tom, we're already here and I know Janie will just love it." She clasped her hands together in anticipation. "Go ahead Janie, open it."

Deciding to be gracious, Janie began to peel the tape away. She hardly got started when something huge, orange and furry exploded from inside. It was a massive tabby cat. He hit the counter looking from one person to another as if he was sizing up his domain and its occupants. His focus keyed in on Janie.

"His name is Demon." Laura cackled. "Isn't he magnificent?"

Tom cleared his throat, clearly embarrassed. Kevin merely stared at the hairy apparition, not quite hiding the look of disgust on his face.

Laura looked from Kevin to Janie. Managing to look crestfallen, she wheedled, "Don't you like him?"

"Well we haven't gotten around to discussing having pets yet." Kevin said, not meeting her eyes.

Tom apologized, "That's what I tried to tell her. I knew we should have called and asked you first but Laura was set on surprising you."

"Well you certainly managed to do that!" Janie spat.

"Well if you hate cats that much I suppose I could drive clear back to Chicago and return him. "Laura whined.

Bloody orange eyes blazed at Janie, taking her in from head to toe. He licked his lips as his gaze paused at her waist. Instinctively her hands went to her stomach, to the tiny life growing there. She could not move her eyes from his. She reeled; losing the room. Here was a power more terrifying than she could ever have imagined. One word escaped her lips as she slipped into darkness, "Mom".

She heard her mother's voice then. Soothing and healing it came to her in the void. Shimmering color surrounded her as she felt the caress of that gentle lady. She wanted to speak, but found it wasn't necessary. Her mother spoke within her, telling her the things she would need to know. She understood then that she must listen now. Her body relaxed, her mind opened to receive all that her mother and many before her had kept sacred, to be revealed to Janie when she would need it most.

All that Jenny McGinn had been in life now passed to her daughter Janie. This sharing would have to be enough to save her child and her grand child from the evil that had come to take what was innocent and precious.

When at last Janie's eyelids fluttered open she heard Kevin's sigh of relief. She was lying in bed with Kevin keeping watch over her. She smiled. Dear, sweet man. He looked so worried. She raised a cold hand to his cheek. He held it there, kissing her palm.

"Janie Kay Miller, you scared the hell out of me! Until Dr. D pronounced you perfectly sound, I thought I would lose my mind!" He choked.

"The doctor was here?"

"Of course he was here. You folded like a tent when you saw that freaky cat! Christ! I will never forgive Tom or that bag for bringing that filthy thing to our home. What the hell was he thinking? People don't just give other people animals without asking them first. And even if they did, why the hell would anyone pick out a flea bitten, ugly thing like that?" He shouted.

Stroking his arm Janie asked calmly, "Where is the cat now Kev?"

"What? Oh, I don't know. I was so worried about you I didn't think to look for it. Tom and Laura left in a hurry. He had Laura's arm in a death grip on the way to the car. I imagine the fireworks are in full swing with those two about now. I'd say it was a long time coming! I never could see what he found so attractive about that bitch! If she isn't pushing him into something, she's pulling him around by the nose. Either way, he can't call his soul his own when she's around."

Janie felt a tug at the corner of her mouth. "Oh my darling man," she thought, "If only you knew how close to the truth you actually are." But she said nothing as he continued his tirade. She let him unload without interruption. All these years he'd kept quiet about Laura to spare his friend. But this was too much. He stopped mid-rant, feeling like an idiot. Here she was pregnant with his child, fresh from a fainting spell, and instead of being supportive and soothing he was shouting like a mad man.

His rage had been instant. His Janie was in some sort of danger. Nothing in this world mattered but Janie and the baby. He would kill, if necessary to preserve that precious nucleus of his heart and soul.

Quiet now, he smiled at her. "I'm such a fool. The last thing you need right now is a raving lunatic for a husband." She held out her arms where the fear and anger quickly melted away. Who was comforting who? She insisted on joining him making a sweep of the house for the cat, but he did not want to be found. Wherever he was hiding, he was good at it. When they finally gave up and went to bed, they shut and locked the bedroom door, something they had never done before.

When Janie woke up the morning was well on its way to becoming afternoon. She dare not open her eyes as she grasped furtively for the thing receding from her mind. She knew a truth, something vital. It was there in the fleeing darkness. "Please wait." She whispered, but it was gone.

As she dressed, she tried once more to reclaim that moment of knowledge that escaped her. Nothing surfaced. She felt languid and slow, shuffling along the carpet and out to the living room. Kevin's pajamas lay on the sofa. He must have dressed out here to keep from waking her. She smiled as she picked them up. Her wonderful husband. She hugged the material to her. He was so considerate of her, so thoughtful. He had held her so tenderly last night after the incident with the cat.

Time stood still. Her heart fluttered, and for a moment seemed to stop beating. The cat! Was it still here or had Kevin found it and taken it with him? Cautiously she began a slow walk through the house. She didn't have to search long. The cat was lying on the counter below the kitchen witch, his eyes studying her as she entered the room.

"Hello you menace from hell. How would you like to take a little ride with me this morning?"

She approached the counter with the intention of putting him back in the box he had come in, and then transporting him to the humane society. Tentatively she reached out her hand to calm him with a few strokes. His eyes followed her hand as it came closer to his head. A barely audible sound rumbled up from inside him. Instinctively she stopped her forward momentum. It may have been a purr, or it may have been a growl. She wasn't sure. She did not want to be bitten.

Now what? She was afraid to grab him; sure he would bite if she tried. Great! Now she knew where he was, but she didn't know what to do about it.

"I guess I could call Animal Control and pretend he just walked in here on his own." She muttered to herself. Yet she felt that it would take more than Animal Control to rid them of this thing. How much more she wasn't sure.

Once again she tried to tap in to that dark well of knowledge she knew was just beyond her consciousness. She knew things, skills that were hers if she could open that locked door in her mind. This creature before her was much more than just a cat. To rid herself of it she would need help.

Demon raised his huge head to stare at her. He knew what she was thinking. She reached for her cell phone. The cat sprung from the counter knocking the phone from her hand. When she tried to grab it, he hissed and scratched a deep welt on her arm. Droplets of blood began to blossom from the narrow wound. She pulled a linen dish towel from the drawer and retreated to the bathroom for iodine and bandaging. Aside from his other threats, this guy was a good bet for disease or infection.

Demon stood in the doorway watching her clean and bandage the scratch. She looked directly into his eyes. She did not flinch as she warned him, "You would do well to remember that I am not alone you spawn of hell."

A flicker of doubt flashed in his eyes. He lowered his head and turned away from her. When she looked into the kitchen a few minutes later, the cat was lying on the counter under the madly spinning witch. She reminded herself that Demon was also not alone. There could be no room for mistakes, no margin for error. For now they were at an impasse. Perhaps tonight they would be able to corner the animal and get rid of him. That was the thought that she maintained every night for weeks.

They tried everything they knew how to do to trap the cat. Kevin finally resorted to calling Animal Control from his office. A growing fear for Janie and the baby prompted him to ask for their help. When Kevin got home that night the house looked like a bomb went off. Janie was sitting stiffly in the recliner, pale and shaking.

"What in hell happened in here? Did Animal Control do this?" He demanded.

Janie raised her tear filled eyes to his. His heart melted. He held her tenderly, letting her sob quietly into his shoulder. How could he be so callous? The ordeal must have been horrendous to cause this much of a mess. Gently he pulled her from his shoulder so he could see her beautiful face.

"At least the sun of a bitch is gone honey." Relief was evident in his voice.

Tearfully she nodded. "They finally had to dart him." She said. "There was no other way. He bit both men and shredded some of their clothes into the bargain."

"Don't worry about the mess baby; I'll call Cindy and Katie. They would love to help and the three of you can always find a way to have a good time when you get together."

Kevin held her close until she was quiet and not shaking. He suggested they get cleaned up and go out for dinner. On the way to the restaurant, he called Cindy and Katie and asked them to join them for dinner. They happily agreed.

Over shrimp appetizers, Kevin told the girls about the beast that Laura had foisted on them and the trouble it had caused. Katie, always the outspoken one raised the question, "why the hell don't you make Laura *LaStrange* come over and clean up the mess? She's the cause of it all!" But Cindy chimed in with, "because she would have to put up with the bitch while she was here, that's why!" They all nodded their agreement.

Both the girls immediately volunteered to help set the house in order. All in all it was a pleasant evening. They even managed to laugh and smile before they went their separate ways.

Although Tom had called almost every day to apologize and even offered to take the cat off their hands, they had not seen him since the night Laura brought Demon to their house. Kevin felt a tug at his heart when he thought about his friend and the ugly way he was being used by Laura. He wondered again why Tom could not see her for what she was. Looking across the front seat at his beautiful wife he felt a pang of guilt. Here he was with everything he had ever dreamed of and his best friend in the world had nothing but the torment of his obsession with the bitch from hell.

He resolved to have a talk with Tom soon. Even at the risk of their friendship, Kevin was determined to try to get Tom to see her for what she really was. In any case Laura would not be welcomed back into their lives.

The house felt warm and at peace that night. They slept without dreams. Only bright tomorrows lay ahead for them now.

In the kitchen a white hatred drew strength from its rage. Sweetness and light would prevail this night, but fools beware, tomorrow hell would come calling.

Demon cut a swath through the gentle night with his tail as he lay on the front porch of the Miller's home. His temporary incarceration had done nothing to diminish his resolve to finish the vile task for which he had been summoned. Inside the house, the Millers slept peacefully unaware of the menace waiting just outside their door.

The coffee pot made its little bubbly sounds, the aroma of sausage and potatoes wafted through the room. Kevin's favorite time of the day was morning breakfast with Janie. The deal was, the first one up prepared breakfast for both of them on weekends. Kevin was up.

The aroma and the noise soon brought Janie to the kitchen door. She smiled as she watched him cook. He felt her presence. Her hair was a mess, her pajamas wrinkled, her eyes still sleepy, but that smile lit up the day as it always did.

"I have a confession to make". She whispered. "I've been awake for an hour watching you sleep. I played possum so you would have to cook breakfast".

"I knew you were awake. Janie. I just let you think I thought you were sleeping so I could come out and cook breakfast." He grinned.

"Well I knew you knew I was awake so you could come out and cook breakfast, so there!"

This went on for a few more minutes until they were both laughing.

"I'll get the paper if you'll watch the sausage for a minute, unless of course you want to go back to bed and pretend to sleep for another half hour".

She laughed and threw a dish towel at him. The sausage needed turning, the potatoes needed flipping. She busied herself at the stove, happy to have their lives in peace and order again. Together they could deal with most anything. She sighed. What a beautiful wonderful life they would have together. She could envision them doing the same thing years from now, after the kids were grown and gone. Two old, yet attractive, mustn't forget that, people fixing breakfast together.... Her reverie was interrupted by a resounding, "What the bloody hell!?" from the front door.

Before she could react a yellow ball of matted fur streaked past her, heading for the living room. At the same time something else registered in her mind. The kitchen Witch had begun to spin. She had nearly forgotten the damn thing. While all of this was filling her mind, Kevin shot past her chasing the cat. One more thought before joining him in the pursuit. "How did he get here?"

The cat crouched on the fireplace mantle, his teeth and claws at the ready. A low moaning growl exuded hatred. Kevin grabbed the closest thing he could get his hands on, the fire place poker. Janie gasped when he took a swipe at the cat, missing but getting a deep scratch on his wrist from Demon's claws.

 "Kevin, stop!" She screamed. "Let's call Animal Control again, please!" she pleaded.

"What the hell for. He'll just come back again. I'll knock him out and take him to the vet to be euthanized. That'll end it once and for all."

The cat stood, arched his back and flew off the mantle at Kevin's face. Luckily Kevin ducked enough that the cat only skimmed his shoulder. Now running for the bedroom, the cat left a trail of urine as he flew past them. The smell was disgusting. Janie turned her head away holding her nose. She saw a ribbon of smoke coming from the kitchen. The breakfast was burning!

She ran to the kitchen to turn off the burners, but stopped short in the doorway. Above the counter the kitchen Witch was bobbing up and down like a cork in the ocean. Janie was almost certain the ugly thing was laughing, could almost hear it cackle. Kevin pushed by her frozen body to pull the pans from the stove and drop them in the sink. He started to ask her why she hadn't done it but the look in her eyes silenced him. Her full attention was on the kitchen Witch. He was puzzled as he looked from Janie to the

Witch. She acted as though she were hypnotized. The Witch hung quietly from her thread of silver, as inanimate as it was supposed to be.

He took her shoulders and cut off her line of vision with his face. He spoke gently to her. "Janie, honey what's the matter? Come on baby snap out of it. The cat is locked in my closet. He won't bother us anymore. I'm going for a cage and then I'll take it to the vet to have it euthanized. The damn thing is too mean to live with anyone".

He took her in his arms as you would a child, speaking softly. "When all this is over I'm going to call Tom and explain very carefully why he can never bring that Bitch of his over here again." He promised her nothing like this would ever happen again. Recognition dawned in her eyes. She nuzzled his neck and tightened her grip on him. She knew she should feel reassured but her heart was caught in an iron vice of fear and foreboding. She wanted to tell him that it wasn't over. She opened her mouth to warn him, but could not speak.

He laid her gently on the couch promising to be right back, and he was. He had his phone in hand and dialed Animal Control first. They were sorry but no one was available on Saturday mornings but if the animal was a threat he should try calling 911. Kevin wanted to jump through the phone and strangle the idiot on the other end. He calmed himself for Janie's sake, dialed the vet, and then the Police. The policeman on duty told Kevin to call Animal Control. He explained the situation and that no one from Animal control was available. He explained that the cat was out of control and probably rabid. He told them he had it locked in a closet and that he was going for a live trap, could they meet him at his house

P a g e | 88

in half an hour. The vet had promised to euthanize the wild cat as soon as he brought it in.

The officer finally agreed to dispatch a car to their address but said it would be at least a half hour before he got there. Kevin thanked the officer profusely and hung up.

Satisfied he had things under control he promised Janie he would only be fifteen or twenty minutes. He had to go to the hardware store and get a live trap.

She heard herself keening a high pitched wail. "Noooooooooo! Please don't leave me here with them!"

Curiously he asked her what she meant by *them.* She clutched at him, pulling on his shirt. "Please don't leave me Kevin!" she begged. "Don't you see what they're doing? They want us, the baby and me!"

A chill swept over him as he looked into the eyes of a mad woman. She was unhinged. All of this and the strain of the pregnancy had been too much. Desperate he crushed her to him.

"Janie, Janie please honey, please come back to me. I promise not to leave you ever. I will protect you sweetheart, I promise, I promise."

He rocked her in his arms, stroking her hair, whispering to her, praying at the same time for God to intervene for them. He could hear the cat tearing up the closet door, yowling to get out. What the hell was happening to them? Carefully he took her arms from around his neck. There was no way he could leave now. Someone else would have to go for the cage.

The only person he knew who could help him now was Tom. He had to be careful how he worded this to his friend. Laura could have no part in it.

He tried to sound normal and jovial on the phone. He asked what Tom was doing this morning and held his breath. He sagged with relief when Tom told him he was just sitting around waiting for Laura to come home. She was out shopping or something with her friends.

"Listen Tom, I need you to go to the hardware store and get a live trap and bring it over to my house. Please don't ask any questions, just trust me. Can you do that for me buddy?"

Tom figured it must be for Demon. He also knew Kevin well enough to know that the matter was urgent and figured he'd understand when he got there.

"I'm on my way out the door! Just hold tight I'll be there in twenty!"

Kevin let the breath he'd been holding escape in a long sigh. Help was on the way. Janie moaned and whimpered. He tried to reach her but she seemed to be in some sort of trance. "Please baby, please hear me."

His next call was to their doctor. He got an answering machine with instructions to call 911 if this were an emergency.

The cat began to scream. The hairs on the back of Kevin's neck prickled at the sound. It almost sounded human! In the kitchen the Witch no longer hung from her silver cord, she walked the length of the counter with a confident stride and took flight. Demon must be freed before anyone or anything could interfere with her plans.

Kevin shivered. The temperature in the house had dropped at least twenty degrees. He wanted to get a blanket to cover Janie with but dared not leave her. She continued to whimper, mumbling incoherently.

Only a few words were discernible. She cried out, "Please don't hurt my baby!"

"Who are you talking about Janie? Who wants to hurt our baby? Nothing is going to hurt the baby honey. The cat is locked up and the police are on their way. Tom is bringing a live trap so we can get rid of the cat once and for all. Please Janie; it's only a demented cat!" Even as he spoke the words, he felt that it was more than that, much more.

With his free hand he dialed 911. He was sure Janie needed to go to the hospital. She had to get through this. He refused to see it any other way.

The phone was dead. It still had plenty of bars, but it wouldn't work. Janie's cell was across the room. He untangled himself and grabbed her phone. Nothing. He still had the land line he kept for office use.

Silently praying, he picked up the handset. Dead. He dropped it into the cradle. How was this possible?

"It's Laura", she muttered. "They're coming for us, they're coming now!"

The noise from the closet suddenly ceased. Janie had grown quiet and still. Instead of relief, Kevin felt terror stricken. Something was about to happen, something unimaginable. He felt it in his gut; he knew it in his heart.

Janie had begun to writhe on the couch. He picked her up to carry her to the bedroom thinking she would be more comfortable there. As he did so he realized her water had broken. A mixture of blood and placental fluid soaked through her clothes into the couch.

"The baby is coming Janie!" She seemed not to hear him. He laid her on the bed and went for a warm wash cloth to bathe her face.

Twenty minutes passed, then thirty. The police didn't come. Kevin kept checking the phones, they were all dead. "Where the hell were they?" he wondered.

Kevin had no way of knowing that everyone he called forgot the conversation the minute the phone connection was broken. No one was coming to help them, no one.

Desperately he scanned the room. He tried to remember what he would need to deliver the baby if no one showed up. His eye focused on the closet door. It was open. The interior of the closet was nothing but tattered clothing. The inside of the door had been flayed of its paint.

His mind grasped for clarity. The cat was free. He wouldn't even attempt to rationalize the situation by telling himself it was only a cat. His eyes darted around the room. No cat. He left Janie only long enough to close and lock the bedroom door. She was moaning louder now, gripping the brass headboard and wincing in pain.

"Janie, how close are the pains?" he asked her.

Her eyes flew open. "Kevin the baby is almost here!" She screamed. "Don't let them have her please! Promise me!" She begged.

"Nothing or no one will touch our baby Janie. I swear it to you."

Janie didn't hear him now. Reality fled as she retreated into darkness where he could not follow. Her breathing was barely detectable. He thought for one terrified moment that she was dead. He realized he was crying and wiped the tears from his face. He had to pull it together for all their sakes.

Carefully lifting her knees, he pulled her soaked pajama bottoms off. More fluid and blood flowed from between her legs. He pushed her knees apart to see if the baby was ready to come out. The baby's head was crowning. Time was short. He placed a pillow under each knee to keep his line of sight unimpeded. He got towels and sheets from the linen closet and pushed them under her. He could see the contractions pushing the baby further. He looked at Janie. She was unaware of what was happening.

"Janie you must help me honey please! I need you to push baby. Push as hard as you can. Our little girl is almost out. Wake up Janie, we both need you!" He cried.

Janie's head turned. Her eyes looked directly at him but remained unfocused. He held her face in his hands pleading with her to come back to him. He put his head against her breast crying softly. He felt lost. He had no choice; he must try his best to deliver their child. He tried to think of everything he had ever heard about child birth. He would need thread or string to tie off the umbilical cord and scissors to cut it with. He supposed all these things needed to be sterilized but settled for pouring rubbing alcohol over everything.

Returning from the bathroom he stopped dead in his tracks. There at the foot of the bed was Demon and he was not alone. With a tiny hand on Janie's foot the kitchen Witch stood staring with rapt attention at the struggling newborn. Her eyes locked on to his and his world ceased to exist. He dropped the things in his hands and lowered himself slowly into a chair. His eyes glazed over, he lost understanding of what was happening in the room. What few remnants of Kevin Miller's mind that remained could not help his wife or his unborn child.

The only sounds in the room now were the groans of the woman on the bed in the throes of labor.

The baby's shoulders could be seen now. The Witch was throbbing with excitement. Laura's eyes looked out through the tiny opaque marbles of the kitchen Witch. She would not be denied her moment of triumph. Centuries of planning and manipulating the weak and useless brought them to this moment. As far as anyone would know, the happy couple would deliver their own baby for lack of time, and the three of them would live their idyllic lives in peace and harmony. But the eyes that looked out from Janie's face would be Laura's.

The baby that grew and flourished under their care would harbor another inside its perfect little body. Kevin would at last belong to Laura, body and soul. This is what she had made her bargain for. Any sacrifice she had ever made was worth the payoff she was soon to claim. Janie had merely been an incubator for the child they needed to seal the agreement.

The child was within seconds of being born. Janie's heart beat had begun to slow, her breathing labored. The Witch crept closer. The demon offered a warning growl. Not yet, be patient. Janie's heart stopped. Her body relaxed into the bedding. The child was born!

Kevin's mind fought for control. So intent was the Witches concentration on the child that her control of him had weakened. His heart burst with pain as he realized that his Janie was gone but his focus went immediately to the tiny baby fighting to take her first breath. With every fiber of his being he fought to move his body. His only desire was to save the child from the evil creatures on the bed. Tears poured from his eyes as he was forced to accept that he would not be able to save either one of them.

A sharp intake of breath and the first cry from the baby filled his heart. He closed his eyes then. He was defeated. His head fell forward on his chest. It was finished.

The baby cried out again and was joined by the cackle of the Witch and the purr of the cat. The Witch began to spin around as if she were still suspended on her silver cord. The cat swung its tail in a swift arc, purring louder still. A celebration of sounds filled the room, a cacophony of evil profound and victorious.

The cat inched closer to the infant. The Witch began to shake with anticipation. But a moment and the cat would be no more. Demon and infant would be one. The child wailed louder. Even in its infancy the child sensed the approaching evil. Laura, the Witch clasped her hands together cackling with unfettered joy. Faster and faster she spun in her circle, waiting, screaming for the finish to be realized.

Silence filled the room like a tidal wave. Kevin opened his eyes. The Witch was still. The cat had stopped purring. Even the child was still and quiet. It was as though the world had paused for a moment in time, waiting for what he could not fathom. The still form of his Janie began to move. Her chest rose with a breath, her eyes opened and cleared The cat arched his back as the Witch retreated a few steps.

There was a sound present that only Janie could hear. It was a whisper of words carried by an underlying din he could not yet identify.

"Mom" she whispered, her smile radiant.

"I'm here Janie. It's time for you to remember. You must use all your will, all your powers, everything you have been taught to save your husband and your child. The evil before you has followed us long before you or I came into this world. It now comes to this; you have what you need to prevail against them, you need only to search your mind and heart for the knowledge you already have. I and those who came before me will help you. They're coming Janie! Hear them?"

Somewhere in his sub-conscious Kevin recognized the sound. He was suddenly thrust back in to the past. He was eight year old Kevin Miller, the new kid on the block. He was in a glade of trees waiting for the dragon lady to arrive.

She was here with them now. Thousands of wings beating in unison surrounded him. Janie and the baby were enclosed in that living force as it settled itself between them and the two beings on the bed.

The Witch began to spin once more, a black putrescence emanating from her wake. She shrieked as she spun round and round. As she spun the cat was changing shape and color. From a tabby orange it had become a fiery red. It stretched and grew in different directions until it no longer resembled a cat. Demon looked more like a bat now, a bat with claws and scales, a vision straight out of nightmares.

The Witch was now a blur, still shrieking wildly. The dragonflies began to glow. Like opals in the sun they glowed with all the colors in the world at once. Janie crossed her arms over her breasts, soft murmurings coming from her lips. The light became brighter with each word she uttered.

The red entity on the bed grew opaque and shimmered. One moment it was terrifyingly real, the next it was fading into nothingness. The Witch suddenly stopped its insane spinning. Its eyes as black as space itself locked on to Janie and the baby. Slowly Janie rose from the bed. The same aura of color emanated from her body. She looked down at the Witch and the bat with disdain. She spoke directly to the witch.

She swept her hand in their direction. A legion of voices joined hers. "You are commanded to return to the hell from which you came! You have no power here anymore!"

Kevin heard the words clearly. The voices seemed to resonate from the wings of the dragonflies.

The words pierced the Witch like a knife. She shrieked again. The demon vanished without a sound.

The Witch screamed and spat foul words at them. With a great effort she tried to come nearer the child, but the evil that drove her was gone. In a blink of time not even the hand crafted witch doll remained.

When next Kevin opened his eyes Janie was snuggling in the bed with a lustily crying baby girl. Her face was red and crinkled and beautiful. There was nothing and no one else in the room. Janie was more radiant than he had ever seen her. Something tugged at his memory, something dreadful. He tried in vain to regain the fast retreating thoughts but could not. His eyes were filled with his wife and child. The peace and love that filled the room were all that survived.

He was exhausted after he and Janie had delivered the baby together. There hadn't been enough time for them to get to the hospital. He bent to kiss the babies downy head and share a kiss with Janie before calling 911. The voice on the other end answered in just a few seconds. They were on their way. Looking at the two of them he knew they were both just fine. He had done all right for a novice daddy.

For only a moment he thought he saw something in her eyes. Something ancient and knowing seemed to look back at him from their depths. The tableau of this night would only remain in her memories, to be passed on to her daughter if there was ever a need.

She laid a hand on his arm and smiled her cure-all smile and everything was fine and normal. A caress as soft as a silken wing brushed away all that was disturbing from his world.

Eight years later:

Cory Daniels was the new kid on the block. Like an idiot he was waiting in the woods for a woman to show up who could call dragons from the sky. Of course he couldn't back down from the dare the other boys had challenged him with, so here he was. He pretty well had himself convinced that the joke was on him when he heard footsteps.

Mrs. Miller, the "dragon lady" had arrived.

The Marmon

Robert Sydney Thomas was four years old when the Marmon came. From a dim corner of his room the Marmon stared at him in silence. He wondered at its appearance. Far from the green, scaly dragon or huge hairy monster that other children imagined, the Marmon was small, no larger than a house cat. Luminescent tear shaped eyes blinked in the darkness. The Marmon tried not to fidget, waiting for Robbie's invitation to climb on the end of the bed, there to curl up and sleep at his feet.

Robbie grinned as the Marmon began to squirm, much like he did half way through the pastor's sermon that morning in church. The glow from the street lights caught the silky softness of its red fur and for a moment as its head refused to be still lit its eyes like beacons. One of the things Robbie liked best about the Marmon was its eyes. Eyes that glowed with nothing but love for him all the time, not just when he was a good boy but even when he wasn't.

Robbie chuckled as the Marmon began to pick at the fur on its fat little tummy. It began to swing its short legs in a widening circle. Like Robbie, its legs were not long enough to reach the floor when sitting on a chair. Its tiny hands also resembled Robbie's, except that his didn't end in long shiny nails like the Marmon's did.

Patting the bed Robbie waited for the warm tingle that began in his feet as the Marmon settled there. No other pet or human being had ever made him feel so warmly safe and loved. He vaguely remembered a big smelly dog that used to sleep in his room when he was younger. It wasn't really his dog though; it was his dad's dog long before Robbie was born.

One morning when Robbie woke up the dog wouldn't open his eyes. His dad told him the dog had gone to heaven. Robbie didn't miss him much. He was old and tired and never wanted to run and play. The Marmon always wanted to do exactly what Robbie wanted to do. The Marmon never got tired of having fun. The Marmon was his very best and truest friend. And best of all, no one in the whole wide world had a Marmon but Robert Sydney Thomas.

Robbie closed his eyes with a contented sigh. No unhappy thought or unpleasant thing could enter Robbie's world now. The Marmon protected him from those things. As Robbie drifted into sleep not even the thought of the empty bed in the morning upset him. For tonight, for right now, the Marmon was with him.

Sunlight filtered through the opening in the curtains and began its journey across the room. A thin finger of light touched the corner where the toy box stood open and overflowing with five years worth of collectables. It moved on to the open closet door where clothes lay in unidentifiable heaps, destination laundry, never reached. Creeping slowly toward the bed, pausing briefly to illuminate two over turned shoes, it traveled on and began to climb. As it touched the foot of the bed it grew in length and warmth reaching for the sleeping boy. He stirred.

Though awake, Robbie kept his eyes tightly closed. As he did every morning since the marmon came he made the same fervent wish. With all his being he wished that this morning he would open his eyes to find that the marmon had not gone with the night. Cautiously he wiggled his toes, stretching further down the bed. An empty little pocket of warmth was the only thing left to let Robbie know that the marmon was real, but alas, he was gone.

His disappointment lingered but a moment for he knew that with the night the marmon would return. He smiled his happy smile and went down to breakfast with his dad and his aunt Suzan. Both smiled as he joined them. Dad ruffled his hair and went back to his paper. Aunt Suzan dished him up some scrambled eggs, asked him how he slept and went back to her sink full of dirty dishes.

As he ate his eggs he could feel his dad and aunt Suzan looking at him when they thought he wasn't watching. He was very young but he thought he understood why they kept doing that. He felt those worried side-long looks since his mother had gone to heaven a few months ago. It was as if they were waiting for him to do something, but he couldn't figure out what. Eric and Suzan always had wrinkle frowns these days. They didn't talk much either. The only sound in the room was the rustling of dad's paper and the dishes clanking together in the sink. It was the same every morning. Robbie sat back from his empty plate. As if on cue his dad laid aside the paper and leaned closer. As he opened his mouth, aunt Suzan pushed between them to fill his coffee cup. A tickle of fear made a quick circle in Robbie's tummy. Dad and Suz stared at each other. Her eyebrows climbed up her forehead as her head moved from side to side. Robbie relaxed. Dad wouldn't remind him of the bad thing this morning. Dad sighed, slumping in his chair. A few minutes later he was on his way out the door with aunt Suzan telling him not to miss his train.

Robbie decided this would be a good day. And tonight the marmon would come and make it a good night. Quietly he pushed his chair from the table and tip-toed from the room before aunt Suz could wrestle him into a sweat shirt and warm jacket. The sun was warm and sweet on his face. From his back yard he could see Jamie two doors away playing with his dumb dog, George. Spotting Robbie he called out, "Hey Robbie come and see what George just learned to do!"Robbie pasted a smile on his face as he crossed the neighbor's yard. Inside he was not very happy to see that Jamie was out with George. He hated George and George didn't like him very much either.

As Robbie shuffled into Jamie's yard, George, who had been happily chasing a Frisbee, turned his huge body so fast in his direction it startled him. Instantly George's upper lip pulled into a snarl.

"Stop that!" Jamie yelled, but the dog had already begun to walk slowly toward Robbie. He growled as he advanced on the terrified boy. Robbie began to back away, never breaking eye contact with the dog. From the corner of his eye he could see a baseball bat lying just to his left. Slowly he knelt and picked it up.

Desperate to protect both his dog and his friend, Jamie threw himself at the advancing dog. Taken by surprise, George instinctively snapped at the intruder and found himself with a mouth full of his master's arm. All hell broke loose. Robbie hit the dog on the rump with the bat, Jamie howled in pain, the dog yowled in surprise, and through the melee' someone was screaming at the top of their lungs. It took a second or two for Robbie to realize it was him.

The door to Jamie's house burst open and two terror stricken adults joined in the fracas, grabbing the boy, kicking the dog, shoving Robbie out of the way and yelling at everyone. Other neighbors began to appear, wondering what all the excitement was about. Suddenly people were everywhere, all talking at once, and nobody listening to anybody. Robbie was in no way in the spotlight. The concern at the moment was the bloody wound on Jamie's arm and the whereabouts of the now vicious George. Robbie took this moment to make his escape.

Late that afternoon a heavy rain kept Robbie inside and sulking. There was nothing good on television, no one to play with, and no marmon till tonight. As he stared out through the rain coated window he saw a bedraggled George sneaking back into Jamie's back yard. Fleetingly he wondered again why George hated him so much.

Robbie wondered about a lot of things. For instance; he wondered why his aunt looked so terrified when he met her at the back door, and why was she was shaking. She kept asking him what happened, like it was his fault or something. He was kind of annoyed but also a little scared. A creepy crawly little thought tried to worm its way in. Suz looked like that other time, that other time when his mom……

He began to shiver. This was an icy cold that didn't come from outside. He shook his head. He wouldn't let the bad thing come out. The bad thing wasn't part of him. No! No! No!

Suzan recognized the signs. She spoke softly, soothingly as she gathered him to her. He felt himself stiffen in her arms. The air rushed out of him. His body went limp and without understanding why he began to sob. Suzan's arms were comforting. Her tears mingled with his as they gave themselves up to an outpouring of pain and loss. Then just as suddenly as it had begun it ended. Aunt Suzan released him, wiped a last tear from her cheek and walked quickly into the house without a backward glance.

Confused and empty Robbie followed silently behind. If asked why he had sobbed so hard he would have no answer. This emptiness he felt had no beginning or end, it just was. All afternoon aunt Suz tried to bring him out of his sullen mood. She put milk and cookies on the table in front of him but he just stared at them with a puzzled look on his face.

Robbie so wanted to sit back and relax, stuff himself with his aunt's chocolate chip cookies and feel happy again. He felt something closing over him like a thin grey shroud. The bad feeling wouldn't be wished away. Aunt Suz put a hand on his shoulder.

"Are you o.k. honey?"

Robbie looked at her hand. A cold chill passed from the boy to the woman. She drew back instantly. His eyes were empty. She tried again.

"Robbie honey, can't you tell me what's bothering you? Please try. Your dad and I have been very worried about you. If you and I could just talk a little about your mother..."

She got no further. Robbie's eyes focused on her face. Feelings, memories warred for a forward position in his mind. His mouth tried to form words but when he tried to talk, when he tried to get it to come out, make it real, when he tried to say it out loud, he opened his mouth and vomited on the kitchen floor.

Suzan jumped to her feet reaching for a dish towel. Running cold water on the towel, her eyes never left his face. He had not moved. He just sat there staring at the mess on the floor. She gently wiped his mouth with the damp towel and eased him from the chair toward the bathroom. He remained silent while she removed his soiled clothing and put clean pajamas on him. He went through the motions of lifting his arms and legs for her but it was as if he were sleep walking.

She put him in bed, tucking the sheets around him. As she bent to kiss him he burst into tears. She sat on the edge of the bed gently rocking him in her arms until his breathing was regular and she knew he had fallen asleep. Suzan was no doctor but she knew in her heart of hearts that there was something horribly wrong with this child that she cherished as if he were her own. He was all there was left of her beloved sister, Marie. She made up her mind to call Eric, Robbie's dad. He always knew what to do. He could always take charge and make things all right again. That was just one of the many reasons why her sister Marie had loved him so much, and why she loved him even more.

Suzan had always been in love with Eric. But Eric was Marie's husband. Suzan did the right thing for all of them in moving many hundreds of miles away to attend college. If Marie ever wondered why Suz didn't come back home to teach after graduation, she never voiced it. Maybe she knew deep down how Suzan felt. Maybe she sensed Suzan's torment and understood her flight. Even all these years later and even though she had never told a soul how she felt about Eric, she still felt guilty. And now Marie was gone.

Suzan had put her life on hold to come back and help Eric and Robbie get their lives into some semblance of normalcy. She had to shake these feelings of guilt and concentrate on helping them get through their grief. Her own grief, her guilt, her loves and losses would have to wait. When Eric and Robbie were back on their feet there would be time for her, time enough and more. A wave of loneliness swept over her.

Someday she would have to leave the two people she loved most. They would heal. She never would.

Suzan gave herself a mental slap. How could she be thinking about her feelings when this child was in so much trouble? He didn't seem to register that he'd had a mother, not to mention that she was dead. Worst of all he had been in the room, had witnessed her death, and could not remember any of it. She felt a chill as a picture of her sister's broken body flashed before her eyes. Nothing could have prepared her for that. Nothing.

Robbie's eyes opened slowly. The familiar warmth at his feet told him the marmon was there. The room was dark. Robbie had slept the day through. He could hear muffled voices downstairs. The marmon stirred as he pulled his feet from under the covers. He crept out of bed and knelt on the floor. He peered at the marmon in the dim light. The marmon slept on. He smiled down at the creature. Hesitantly he reached out his hand to stroke it. He had never touched the marmon before. The marmon's fur crackled with blue sparks as he stroked it in the darkness.

Robbie stopped mid-stroke. Something was different about his little friend. For one thing it wasn't so little. Puzzled he stood to study the creature he had conjured not so long ago. He didn't think the marmon could change without his wishing it. He had not wished it and was pretty sure he didn't like it. The marmon should be exactly the same as it was when he wished it into existence.

On closer inspection he realized that the marmon's fur was no longer red, but looked almost black against the sheets. He sat on the bed next to his friend to think. He rationalized that it was probably o.k. for the marmon to grow a little, after all he had grown an inch and a half this last year. His dad was proud of him. He should be proud of the marmon. There was no reason for him to be concerned. And wasn't he pleased with himself for finding the courage to pet his little friend at last. His tummy rumbled.

He left the marmon to his dreams and put on his robe to go down to the kitchen. He was suddenly very hungry. The adults stopped talking as he entered the kitchen. It looked like Aunt Suz had been crying again. He sat next to his father.

"I'll get your supper for you honey." She told Robbie, and went to the microwave to heat it up.

"Aunt Suz tells me you had quite a scare this morning at Jamie's house."

When Robbie said nothing Eric moved closer. "She said you weren't feeling well this afternoon. Feeling better now?"

Robbie smiled at them both and nodded his head.

"Well I'm glad to hear it, and I'm glad you weren't hurt.

Mr. Ferguson said Jamie's dog attacked you boys this

morning? Do you want to tell me about it?" When

Robbie didn't answer he went on. "I'm told Jamie only

needed two stitches to close the wound from the dog

bite."

Robbie stared at his lap. Eric and Suzan exchanged a

look. "Look Robbie, I don't want to make trouble

between you and Jamie but I can't just let it go if the

dog has turned mean. I understand Jamie loves his

dog. He won't talk about it. I want you to think about

this. What if the dog had hurt Jamie seriously or

turned on you or any of the neighborhood children?

You wouldn't want that to happen would you?"

Robbie shook his head no but didn't meet his father's

eyes.

"Let me ask you something Robbie, and I want you to tell me the truth. You and Jamie weren't teasing George were you? You boys have to realize that George isn't a puppy anymore. He is an old dog and he doesn't like to play the same rough and tumble games Jamie's older brothers used to play with him. Did you or Jamie jump on him accidently or step on him? I need to know before I speak to Jamie's dad. I would hate to see George put down if all this was just an accident."

Robbie sat rigidly in his chair while his father talked. The rage was coming and there was nothing he could do to stop it now. Upstairs the marmon whined in pain. His body writhed on the bed. Robbie's pain was his pain. He too was helpless to stop what was happening to the boy.

"We didn't do anything to that stupid dog! He just hates me that's all, and I hate him right back! I don't care if he is Jamie's dog, I hope he gets hit by a car and dies!" He spat.

Eric and Suz were speechless as he bolted from the room. He ran up the stairs seething inside. His breathing was so loud and ragged he didn't hear the soft cries coming from the little body on the bed. The pain and hatred transmitted itself from the boy to the marmon. The essence of the creature was seized and torn, re-shaped and torn again. The marmon sensed a change and cried out against it. Its tender heart began to harden. The boy's inner turmoil, his evolving strength of emotion clutched at its core. The shuddering mass on the bed was powerless against the onslaught.

If the boy could have sensed the power of his anguish and hatred and how it was affecting the marmon he would have been terrified. It was now too late to halt the events set in motion by the powers that brought the marmon into the little boy's world.

From the bed Robbie heard a whimper. He turned toward the sound. What he saw there made his jaw drop. Blue sparks danced around the figure on the bed. It cried out again. Robbie ran to his friend. Instinct stronger than fear drove him. He stopped just short of grabbing the marmon in his arms. Even in the darkness of the room he could see the luminescent eyes rolling up at him. In them he saw pain and confusion. Cautiously he reached out and touched the bristling fur.

The thing on the bed no longer bore resemblance to the one Robbie had conjured. This thing was twice the size of his marmon. Its fur was no longer soft, it felt stiff and abrasive. Its eyes seemed to plead with the boy. In a croaking voice Robbie knelt by the bed and whispered, "Marmon what's happening to you?" .

The marmon only turned its head away and whimpered. Robbie was numb with fear. For the remainder of the night he kept vigil in his chair across the room listening to the mournful sounds of the marmon.

Downstairs a sometimes vocal, more often silent battle was being waged between the adults. Both were scared, both were unsure what to do but they knew there was a real danger here of losing their Robbie completely. A helpless, hopeless feeling filled the silence between them. Finally Suzan broke the standoff.

"Eric you know what the psychologist said about shocking the boy. He said Robbie would have to remember everything on his own. If you suddenly do or say anything to bring it all back to him you might damage the natural healing process the doctor talked about. He said the child could be mentally scarred for life. It will come back gradually, a little at a time. A sudden memory shift that brought it all back at once could be cataclysmic."

Eric shook his head. "I know what he said Suz, I hear what you're saying but there's just something not right about the boy. I think he remembers more than he's letting on but how in the hell am I supposed to find out if I can't talk to him about it?"

Suzan's heart gave a lurch. So much pain. She could not shield any of them from it.

"Eric please try to be patient. He will remember. Sometimes I wish I could bury the accident in my subconscious the way he has. We don't have any idea how he will handle it or if he will be able to at all. The child is like a ticking time bomb ready to explode any moment. As horrendous as this has been for us, think how much worse it must have been for him to see it happen right before his eyes. When it does come back it may cost him more than we can ever imagine."

Eric slammed his hand on the table. She jumped. "God damn it Suz! I'm tired of this cloak and dagger crap! And I'm tired of hearing you call it an accident! We don't have any idea what happened that night! For all we know..."

"ERIC! Stop it right now! I know where you're going with this and I won't have it. What ever happened that night wasn't intentional. For God's sake! Robbie is just a little boy. He couldn't have realized what was happening. He doesn't know what happened. I mean, it wasn't anything he did. I'm sure of it. Surely you must believe that!"

Eric's face was a study in misery. He was sick with it. Deep inside them they both knew he would never get over the pain of finding Marie that night. The scene came unbidden as it always did in his weak moments. Marie, broken like a china doll on the kitchen floor, Robbie looking down at her, smiling! No one else was there. Nothing else had been disturbed. Blood covered both of them. There was no weapon to explain the horrible wounds on her body or the ghastly amount of blood. But the most terrible and unthinkable part of it all was the sound of Robbie's maniacal laughter. He could hear it now all these months later. He clapped his hands over his ears.

"Eric! Eric! Come back to me! Please don't go there." Suz pleaded.

She may as well have slapped him. The horrid laughter disappeared. He was back in his home with his sister-in-law. Even as he listened to her talking softly about their future he knew he would be suspicious of his child until the end of his days or until the truth finally surfaced. He knew too that the truth he sought and feared could only come from Robbie.

Robbie. The child they had longed for. The child they had prayed for. It took them five years of marriage to make a baby. They were the happiest people alive when the doctor told them the good news. Their lives would now be complete. But fate is no respecter of dreams. The child was flawed. Robert Sydney Thomas was as beautiful a baby as anyone could ever hope for. Marie was elated with her perfect baby boy. But from the first moment Eric held his son he could sense something was not quite right.

In an effort to assuage his fears he insisted that the baby be checked out by every pediatric specialist in the state. Marie found it adorable that he was such a concerned father. He never shared his feeling of unease with her. He hoped it was just a case of new daddy jitters. But he knew there was more to it than that. As a child he had the gift of perception from an early age. People called it good instincts. They didn't understand it but they recognized that he had it.

He could see in to people's hearts and minds. He could sense even the most carefully masked hatred, lust, or envy. In short he could feel the evil in people that others could not. Lucky for him that he also had the comfort of feeling the beauty of love and sincerity in most people. This gift had helped him through life and led him to his beloved Marie.

Now this gift was more of a curse. As much as he wanted to dispel his fears about his son, he was as certain that he was right. When Robbie was three months old Marie decided it was time to continue her night classes at the University. Eric was nervous at the prospect of being alone and responsible for such a tiny baby but Marie assured him that he would do just fine. Reluctantly he watched her drive away.

Robbie was asleep in his bassinette in the dining room where Eric was working on some contracts and with any luck at all would still be sleeping when Marie got home.

As he worked he began to feel a tingling sensation on the back of his neck. He stretched his neck thinking he had been in one position too long. He settled back to the contract but in a few minutes the sensation started again. He brushed at his neck, maybe a fly or a spider. Then a stabbing pain hit him hard. He grabbed the back of his neck. He had been stung. But there was nothing there. He didn't know why he looked at the baby but when he did he found himself staring into the eyes of an old if not ancient being. A being so malignant that it sent chills into his very soul.

In a millisecond it was gone. A beautiful smiling little baby boy twinkled happily at his daddy from his bassinette. In a few minutes the baby fell into a peaceful sleep leaving Eric thinking that he must have dosed off and dreamed the whole thing. But when he put his hand on the back of his neck it came away with a tiny spot of blood.

For the remaining hours till Marie came home, he sat by his sleeping infant watching and waiting. As the weeks and months passed he convinced himself that he had indeed been stung by some sort of insect as he slept at the table. But then in the years that followed there were other incidents..........

After the confrontation in the kitchen with Suzan, Eric felt drained. He went to bed with a couple of aspirin and fell asleep almost immediately. The squeal of brakes followed by a loud thud brought him upright from his dream. Something was screaming! Eric made the landing in four strides almost colliding with Suzan. Robbie was right behind them. The screams were getting fainter.

"You two stay here. I'll see what's going on." He ordered, but Robbie had already pushed past him and was bounding down the stairs. He threw open the front door. In the street was a small red sedan with a man leaning on its hood. He looked pale and dazed. He was staring down at his front tires. Robbie followed his gaze to the clump of shaggy fur and pooling blood at his feet.

Suzan gasped as she realized that the bloody mound in the street was a dog, Jamie's dog, George! Unconsciously she and Eric found themselves looking from the dog to Robbie. He stood frozen. He didn't know how he felt at that moment. Everything inside was jumbled up. He felt shaky and scared. A soft Oh of surprise escaped him.

He felt his dad's hand on his shoulder as Jamie ran out into the street and fell to his knees beside George. Jamie's screams of anguish told them that George had not survived. Eric pulled Robbie back into the house and shut the door. There was nothing they could do for George or Jamie now. Jamie's parents were with him.

Robbie looked up into his father's eyes. He was confused by what he saw there. His father looked at him as if he was afraid of him. He didn't like his dad to look at him that way, but somewhere inside he also felt powerful. He pulled away and went quietly up the stairs to his room. He wished George would get hit by a car and die! He needed some time to think about this.. He wondered what else he could do and how far he dared to go. One thing was for sure, no one was going to push him around anymore. In the darkness the marmon groaned. He wasn't on the bed anymore.

Eric sat down hard on the bottom step. Suzan took a deep breath before speaking.

"Eric, what just happened was... well... just a remarkable coincidence. You can't think otherwise. Things like this happen every day. Someone says something in the heat of anger and by some stroke of fate, well it just happens."

Eric said nothing. He shook his head slowly.

"Eric please listen to me!" she begged.

"No Suzan." He whispered. "I don't buy it any more than I buy the bullshit about Marie. You and that shrink can rationalize everything that happens around that kid! I can't! Not anymore!"

"He isn't just "that kid" Eric. He's your son. He's Marie's son. She loved him more than life. Robbie didn't have anything to do with either of these things. Children get hurt and scared. They say hateful things they don't mean."

Eric was silent a moment. "Listen to me Suzan. I

remember when I was a kid my dad pissed me off and I wished him dead, but God damn it Suzan, it didn't happen! When that kid opens his mouth and wishes for something it freaking happens! Don't tell me you've conveniently forgotten what happened the night before Marie was murdered?"

There it was, out at last. Murdered. The one word everyone had skated around, avoided saying out loud. No one could rationally say that a woman was accidentally killed when she was found disemboweled with every bone in her body broken. And no one would ever convince Eric that the boy found at her side covered in her blood, laughing like a deranged psychopath had nothing to do with it. The police with its forensic team could find no trace of another human being in the house at the time of the murder. The coroner was baffled at the condition of Marie's body and could not pinpoint the cause of death. At the final inquest he stated that the body seemed to have imploded. He was never taken seriously after that and retired a few months later. The case went in to the unsolved files, there to remain indefinitely.

Both the police and the shrink on the case theorized that Robbie had seen his mother murdered and had buried it inside. Eric had his own theories.

All this raced across Eric's mind as he sat next to Suzan on the stairs. In Robbie's room the marmon was still. In the boundless void from which he came the darkness was rent with a piercing cry. The boy slept peacefully on having no thoughts of the horrors he was manifesting. Where there was once innocence something else awakened.

Dressed and ready for the day, Robbie stepped out into the sunshine. He shivered even though the sun was warm. He had one thing on his mind. He wanted to see Jamie. He screwed his face into a semblance of sorrow and knocked on Jamie's front door. He would have to be careful not to grin when Jamie told him about George. After all Jamie was his friend. He couldn't help it if George was the stupidest dog in the world.

Jamie's mom opened the door. By this time he had managed to squeeze out a tear that rolled down his cheek. Jamie's mom grabbed him up in a cushy hug.

"Oh Robbie it's so nice of you to come over. Jamie really needs his best friend now." She sniffed. She took Robbie to Jamie's room. He was lying on his bed staring at the ceiling. There were tear tracks on his cheeks but he wasn't crying.

"Hi Jamie", he said cheerfully.

Jamie turned his red and swollen eyes to Robbie and burst into tears. Robbie felt a sudden pang of something he hardly recognized. He was ashamed. He didn't like this feeling, wasn't sure how to deal with it. He mumbled something to the effect that he was sorry about George and ran all the way home. He spent the day in his room trying to sort out a variety of thoughts and feelings that he didn't understand.

Day ebbed into night and the marmon came. The marmon did not sleep with Robbie this night. The marmon could not sleep in Robbie's bed anymore because he was now too large. This marmon would never fit in anyone's bed ever again.

Robbie woke early the next day. He hadn't slept very well. All night he wrestled with his feelings. By morning he was even more confused. He knew

George was dead on account of him and he felt sorry for Jamie because he was very sad. At the same time he was all mixed up with feeling glad that George was gone and wouldn't growl at him anymore or hog any of Jamie's time.

He stepped out on the patio to see if Jamie was outside. Something caught his eye. In the middle of the tulip garden there was a little grey kitten. Its huge green eyes looked up at him trustingly. The cat didn't run away as he approached it which surprised him. Animals didn't seem to like him much. Happily this cat seemed to like Robbie and this pleased him. Just lately he wasn't as excited as he used to be to see the end of the day and the coming of the marmon. He went back in the house, pilfered a bowl, filled it with milk and snuck it out to the cat.

Suzan saw him going out the door with the bowl and followed him to see what he was up to. The sight of the cat made her happy that Robbie had a new friend but sad because she knew what Eric would say about it. Eric knew that Suz was terribly allergic to animals and would insist it be taken to the pound. How she wished she had Marie's tolerance for animals. Lately she had been sneezing a lot. Maybe Robbie had been feeding the cat on the sly for awhile. Robbie smiled as he stroked the purring kitten. He was thinking maybe this would be a good day after all.

Suzan turned back to her kitchen with a wistful look. Had it only been a few short months ago that this house had been filled with warmth? She hoped that Robbie's display of affection and the cat's acceptance of the boy were portents of things to come. She would try very hard to stay away from the cat and hope her allergies didn't get the best of her.

She sighed as she busied herself with cleaning chores. Only God knew why things happen as they do. Marie was gone, Robbie was emotionally ill and Eric was trying to find someone or something to blame for it all. Still, she mused, time is said to set all things right again. When she looked out again there was no sign of Robbie or the cat. They must have gone off somewhere together. Robbie came in for lunch but made no mention of the cat. Though Suzan kept an eye out for the cat for several days, she never saw it again even though her sneezing seemed to be getting worse. Eric would be the one to find what was left of it weeks later under the hedges surrounding the back porch.

Weeks passed and Robbie was happy again. Jamie and he played together every day with no stupid dog to interrupt them. Aside from a few skinned knees and bruises it was turning out to be a pretty good summer. Things had even gotten better at Robbie's house. Suzan was smiling more and Eric wasn't staring at

Robbie behind his back so much. The only bad thing
was going to bed at night. His marmon wasn't his
marmon anymore. It wasn't growing bigger at least for
now, but it had changed so much he hardly
recognized it.

Ah but the days were fine. He loved getting up in the
morning to shovel in his breakfast and race out the
door. Jamie would be waiting for him. Then one day
Robbie knocked on Jamie's door and no one came.
He brooded in his room till aunt Suz called him down
to eat lunch. He had just started on his chocolate
cookie when he heard squeals of delight in his back
yard. He looked out and to his dismay there was
Jamie and his little sister on their way to his door and
they were not alone. A yellow, squirming, tongue
flopping, tail whipping ball of fur was fighting to
wrench itself from Jamie's arms.

Jamie's face was split in a huge grin. Suzan was delighted when she saw the two children on the patio. She hustled Robbie out the sliding glass door before Jamie and his sister actually came in with the puppy. Robbie understood this. He knew his aunt Suzan couldn't breathe well with an animal in the house.

Robbie's smile was stiff when he went out on the deck, but soon the energetic puppy was all over him too. His face was soaked in dog drool and tiny puppy teeth had left little red tracks all over his arms and legs. For a few hours he forgot to be jealous of his friend's affections for the new pup. For a few hours he shared their excitement and the joy of being a kid with a boisterous puppy chasing them all over the yard. He was truly a happy little boy.

That night when Eric got home Robbie could hardly contain himself. He couldn't chew around a mouthful of food without chattering on about Jamie's puppy.

The mood was light and happy at the dinner table. Then Robbie dropped the bomb.

"Dad can I please have a puppy of my own. I'll take care of it myself and clean up after it. Then me and Jamie could play together and both have our own dogs. Please dad?"

Eric and Suzan exchanged looks. Her face was red. She was miserable. Robbie was ready for the argument.

"Robbie you know your aunt Suzan can't have animals in the house." He held up his hand when Robbie started to interrupt. "I know what you're going to say, that you'll keep it outside in the yard with its own dog house. Am I right?"

Robbie nodded solemnly. How did his dad know what he was going to say?

"Robbie you know as well as I do that it would sneak in or you would sneak it in at every opportunity don't we?"

Robbie's heart sank. He knew there was no use arguing with his father. He would not be getting a puppy or a cat or even a darn gerbil as long as aunt Suz was here. He left the table in tears, his mind racing, and his rage growing. His aunt Suz was a stupid woman. She didn't even have a job. She didn't have any friends or a husband either. All she did was stay home and cook food. He turned to look at her as he left the dining room. For one tiny fragment of time Suzan felt her flesh go cold. Then he pounded up the stairs heading for his room.

Before he got all the way up the stairs Eric called him back. He had seen the look in his son's eyes. An icy finger ran down his spine. It hit him suddenly how much having Suzan here mattered to him. The thought that something bad might happen to her was like a vice around his heart.

Robbie stood by the table with his head down. Eric hoped the fear he felt couldn't be heard in his voice.

"Robbie you wouldn't want anything bad to happen to your aunt Suzan would you? You wouldn't want her to be sick or have to leave us?" His eyes pleaded with his son.

Robbie looked at his father and at aunt Suz. His face softened. "No dad. I love aunt Suz."

Eric realized he'd been holding his breath. With a sigh he reached out to ruffle his son's hair, but Robbie ducked under his hand and ran up the stairs. Eric shook his head. It wasn't over then was it?

Suzan began to clear the table. "I'll talk to him again Suz." He said. He touched her hand as she reached for his plate. The contact startled her. She nearly dropped the dish. He looked embarrassed. She tried a smile but it didn't reach her eyes.

"It's all right Eric. He'll brood about it for a few days and be a little put out with me but he'll get over it. Most of the time he'll be too busy with Jamie and the puppy to think about being unhappy. You'll see."

Eric said nothing. His thoughts were racing. He wanted so much to believe that she was right about this. He found he couldn't work that night. Every time he picked up a contract he lost the gist of it within seconds. All he could see were his son's eyes as he stared at Suzan. His heart and mind battled each other. His heart told him he was a fool to even consider what his mind was trying to convince him of. His thoughts raged.

"My son is a monster. He has killed, I know it. I feel it,
He will kill again unless I stop him." But stop him how
was the question. Should he send him away
somewhere? Was there a place for people like
Robbie? Or could he be fixed or cured, made normal?
If none of that would work, could he fix the situation
another way by sending Suzan away? The thought
made him sad, sadder than he thought possible. He
could already feel the emptiness her absence would
leave. But if he kept her here, (a knot of fear gripped
him) could he possibly hurt her? Was she now just
another obstacle in his way?

He knew the boy loved Suzan but he had also loved
his mother didn't he? The same questions, the same
suspicions wouldn't be put down. His head pounding
he dragged himself upstairs to his bedroom. As he
passed Suzan's room he heard her crying softly. He
hesitated for a moment. No he wouldn't intrude. He

fell into a troubled sleep around midnight. Down the hall Robbie wasn't sleeping either. Inside he was seething with rage. He threw things on the floor including all the bedding and hurled himself at the bed. He wanted to scream! He grabbed his pillow and crammed it over his mouth. He shook with anger.

Something brushed his foot. He threw the pillow aside. The marmon had come. His relief that the marmon had grown no bigger was short lived. There were other things. The marmon had something in its mouth. When Robbie got the courage to look closely he could see that they were teeth, long sharp teeth. The marmon's hair was matted and it stunk. Robbie pinched his nose. He covered his face with the pillow and wished the marmon away.

"Go away marmon. I want you to go now. I'm wishing it! Go!" Slowly he lowered the pillow to uncover one eye. The marmon remained. He covered his face and wished harder. But the marmon would not go. It swayed on its grotesquely misshapen legs. Robbie didn't dare look at its eyes; he could feel their warmth on his face.

For the first time Robbie was afraid of the marmon. He had lost control of his creation. The marmon no longer obeyed his wishes. He now realized that he had no idea what the marmon might do. He felt his bladder threaten to release. The truth was that the marmon was no longer his friend.

He jumped out of bed throwing the pillow in the general direction of the marmon. He ran first to the bathroom to relieve himself. As he stood over the commode he tried to compose his thoughts. The marmon was in his room. As far as he knew it couldn't leave his room. Also the marmon could only come at night. If he only went into his room in the daytime he would be perfectly safe. He could sleep in his mom's sewing room. There was a daybed in there. If aunt Suzan insisted on tucking him in he would have a few anxious moments when she shut off the light and closed the door, but the marmon was so big and clumsy now he was sure he could beat it to the door.

His frantic heartbeat began to slow. He relaxed his grip on the sink. He would find a way to get rid of the marmon. Maybe he could wish up another creature to help him get rid of it. Why not? He wished up the marmon didn't he? He could wish up a marmon eating creature that had to disappear immediately after he ate it.

Satisfied with his plan he relaxed. He snuck in to his mom's sewing room. In the dark he talked out loud. "O.K. Marmon! You better have a good time tonight because tomorrow night you're in for a big surprise!"

He chuckled as he concocted an image of the new thing he would wish into existence. He fell asleep with a smile on his innocent looking little face. No one would have guessed how much evil lurked there.

In Robbie's room the marmon shuddered and grew a third eye. A tear rolled from that eye as the marmon mourned for the loss of his little friend, and the loss of himself.

Robbie had been sleeping in his mother's sewing room for three nights now. He hadn't been able to conjure a marmon eater yet but he wasn't giving up. During the day he did indeed play with Jamie and his new puppy just as aunt Suzan had predicted. He was pretty happy with the situation until Jamie announced that he was going to name the new puppy George Junior. Jamie jumped when he heard the puppy yelp. He was limping. He whined when Jamie picked him up. Jamie couldn't see anything wrong with the dog's paws. There were no slivers, bee stings or other injuries, but when he put the pup down he whined louder and fell over.

Robbie could still feel the sting of anger in his belly. George Junior. What a stupid name for a dog! But when Jamie started to cry Robbie felt that guilty pang of shame wash over him again. He knelt by his friend. As his hand stroked the whimpering pup something unexpected happened. George jumped up and bounded away as if nothing had happened. Jamie sat back speechless watching George happily chasing leaves in the wind. He looked at Robbie totally confused.

At first Robbie was confused too, but then an idea took form. Suddenly he knew he had made the puppy well. He could make hurts go away. He found himself beaming at Jamie like a benevolent god. He conveniently forgot that he had caused the puppies'

Injury in the first place. Robbie didn't mind the puppy much after that.

That night he and Suz ate dinner alone again. For several nights running his dad had not come home from work until late at night. Even then he barely spoke to Robbie. He usually went straight to his study weighed down with books he hadn't seen before and then to bed. Robbie didn't mind, he had a lot of things to think about. In fact the more he thought about it the more he decided that his dad was no fun either. He had stupid ideas. He was just as stupid as aunt Suzan. Anger crept up his spine as he remembered why he couldn't have a puppy of his own. His stupid aunt couldn't breathe with animals in the house. So What? He raged. Why should he care if she had to puff on those pipe things of hers? Why should he suffer? It wasn't his fault.

His good humor vanished. He no longer felt good about George Junior either. That dumb dog had no business moving in with his friend Jamie. Maybe he could borrow the dog some night and feed it to the marmon. The thought made him giggle.

Humor restored he decided to go to bed. Aunt Suz wanted to tuck him in. He waited only seconds after she shut his door to jump out of bed. He could feel the marmon's breath on his back as he closed the door behind him.

The stench was getting worse in his room. He hoped no one else could smell it but him. He stood in the hallway outside his door listening to the marmon stumbling around in his room. Curious he opened the door a crack. He couldn't see anything but the stench made him gag.

He opened the door just a tad more. Still nothing. He could hear a rasping noise inside the room. He opened the door still further. When the light from the hallway hit the marmon it whimpered and backed away but not fast enough to go unseen. Robbie could not stop himself from gasping out loud at the sight of it.

The huge black thing in his room in no way resembled his marmon. A gaping maw of a mouth filled with dagger like fangs hung below three red rimmed yellow eyes. Drool hung from the corners of its mouth. The thing could no longer stand on its hind legs and was now attempting to balance on all fours. Long dark claws had grown from its once delicate fingers and toes. As Robbie pulled the door closed a voice came from the thing within. "*R O B B I E.*"

It rasped. The skin on his arms stood upright with

hairy little bumps. This time Robbie shut the door fast.

He scurried to the sewing room and dove in to bed.

He imagined he could still hear that horrible voice

coming from what used to be his marmon. He

shivered under the covers. Holy cow. Of all the scary

things he had imagined to get rid of the marmon,

none of them were up to the task. He was truly scared

that this marmon would hurt him if he gave it half a

chance. Lucky thing it couldn't get out of his room. But

even though he believed it was trapped, he couldn't

help peering into the darkness searching for those

glowing yellow eyes.

Several times in the night he awakened and held his

breath, listening for that grating voice calling his

name. Morning took a long time coming this night.

Robbie was up early as always. He had to get into his

room before anyone else was up. He peeked through

a crack in the door to make sure the coast was clear

before running to his room. Once inside he felt foolish

about last night. The marmon wasn't a real creature.

He was the one who made it up. Make believe things

couldn't really hurt you. He started to feel better about

the whole thing, poor kid.

Just as he was pulling his pajama top over his head

he spotted something on his pillow. He thought he

knew what it was but he hoped he was wrong. When

he touched it he felt his scalp tighten. Marmon hairs,

thick, black and so stiff they nearly pricked his skin

were scattered on the pillow case. There were five of

them. He gathered them up and caught of whiff of

something rotten. The smell was in the hairs and

clung to his pillow. What would aunt Suz think when

she made his bed? Instead of racking his brain for an

explanation he decided to be Mr. helpful this morning

and strip his own bed. He pulled everything off the

bed and dumped it on the floor. It never occurred to

him that the smell would still be on the bedding when she took it to the laundry room to be washed. Something else struck him like a thunderbolt; why were marmon hairs here at all? Shouldn't they be gone in the morning along with the marmon?

He looked at the hairs he had laid on his dresser. He had to dispose of them too. He quickly pulled on his jeans and a t shirt, stuffing the hairs in his pocket. He would scatter them in the yard.

By the time Suzan's bedroom door opened he was coming out of his room with an arm load of bedclothes and a smile on his face. Suzan was surprised.

"What's all this Robbie?"

"I just thought I could help you with the laundry today aunt Suzan."

But Suzan was no fool. She peered at him closely. He looked flushed and sweaty. Maybe he had a bad dream and wet the bed. She thought she may have heard him in the hall a time or two this week. She decided not to embarrass him. "Well thank you Robbie that was very thoughtful."

She started to give him a hand shoving it down the laundry chute. "No I got this." He smiled. As he shoved the last of it down the chute she was suddenly seized with a violent bout of coughing and sneezing. Robbie froze as he watched her body lurching as she struggled to get a breath. Her eyes pleaded for help. He understood immediately. He ran to her room and grabbed her inhaler from her dresser. For a fleeting moment he thought about what would happen if she wasn't around anymore. If she was gone he could probably talk his dad in to getting him a puppy. But Robbie wasn't that far gone yet. He still possessed some vestige of the little boy his mother had loved. The terrible sounds she was making reminded him of the marmon.

He cared about aunt Suz even if she was kind of stupid. He thrust the inhaler into her hand. Moments later she was sitting on the floor gulping air but she wasn't that funny color anymore. She was trying to tell him something but she didn't have enough air to talk. He got in her face and asked if he should call dad. She nodded.

He knew the drill, hit speed dial for his dad's office. Eric answered on the first ring. It was Robbie, not Suzan. A pit of fear opened in his stomach. He heard Robbie say aunt Suz was sick before dropping the phone and running from his office. Robbie starred at the buzzing phone. Without knowing why he was doing it he started to cry. Aunt Suzan was too quiet. Her face was turning a funny color again. He could see the panic in her eyes as she pumped the inhaler.

All at once she dropped it and fell over on her side.

He pushed the hang up button on the phone and

punched in the numbers 911 like his mom had taught

him to do if something really bad ever happened.

Calmly he told the lady on the phone that his aunt

Suzan couldn't breathe. He answered all her

questions about where he lived, how old he was and

stayed on the line just like she told him to do. Aunt

Suzan's eyes were closed now and she wasn't

wheezing. He touched her shoulder and tried to

shake her. She wouldn't wake up. Robbie started to

shake. A ringing in his ears was getting louder. He

couldn't hear himself sobbing anymore. The bad thing

was happening again. The bad thing like before with

his mom. He put his hand over his aunt's mouth and

nose. Little by little he applied more pressure until her

body started to convulse. He felt better. He smiled as

the noise in his head got louder still. He rocked back and forth humming tunelessly. He would go to the bad place now. The bad thing was coming and he was going to the bad place again where he wouldn't see the bad thing happen. He was safe in the bad place.

A thunderous roar erupted from the last vestiges of a soul savagely torn from virtue and hope, to be cast irretrievably into a fiery hell. The marmon passed from the confines of a little boy's sweet imaginings and emerged a soulless embodiment of evil. When the marmon came again it would come from hell of its own accord. A single mindless craving would drive it. This time the marmon would come for a soul.

Eric met the paramedics in the hallway. Suzan was on a stretcher with an oxygen mask over her face, an I.V. in her arm. She was pale and her skin felt clammy to his touch, but she was breathing. Robbie was lying on the floor. His eyes were closed but his eyeballs were revolving madly under the lids as if he were in some sort of violent r.e.m. sleep. A paramedic was speaking softly to him taking his blood pressure.

Eric heard his name being called. A hefty fireman put his hand on Eric's shoulder. It was Terry, a friend of the family. He had been one of the team who came the night Marie died. Terry was telling him that Suzan had suffered an asthma attack, a bad one. He assured him that Suzan would be fine. Eric heard himself ask about Robbie. Terry smiled and clapped him on the back.

"You have quite a boy there Eric. He made the 911 call and did a great job explaining everything to the dispatcher. He saved his aunt's life. I'd be damned proud of him if I were you. As to his present state, the E.M.T. thinks he got terribly frightened and went into shock. He'll be fine. We're taking them both to the hospital trauma center. You can ride along with me if you want."

Eric licked his lips, took a deep breath. "What brought on Suzan's attack Terry? Anybody know?"

Terry shook his head. "Don't know just yet Eric. You know how these things are. Sometimes you never do find a cause."

Eric shook his head. "No, that doesn't make sense. Suzan's particular type of respiratory distress is only brought on by animal hair or dander. We don't have any pets because of it."

Terry could see Eric's emotions were getting the best of him. Small wonder with his losing Marie not that long ago and now this. Still his next question puzzled Terry.

"What was Robbie doing when you got here Terry? Was he touching Suzan at all?"

Terry stared at his friend. "No Eric. Robbie was lying right next her on the floor where he is now. I think he brought her inhaler to her but it must have been nearly exhausted and didn't do her much good. It's empty. I think Robbie panicked when she stopped breathing and went into shock." He put his hand on Eric's shoulder. "Come on buddy I'll give you a lift to the hospital. Trust me they are both fine. "

They rode in silence to the hospital. Eric felt like a cold fist had a grip on his heart. He waited for the doctors to come and talk to him. It seemed like hours had passed when a young intern approached him. He flipped some papers on a chart.

"Is Suzan Keal your sister?" He asked.

"Sister in law." Eric corrected. "I'm Eric Thomas, how is she?"

"Suzan is doing very well Mr. Thomas. She was in severe respiratory distress when she came in. I thought we might have to intubate her but she responded well to treatment. I think we need to keep her few days. But she will be fine."

He scribbled a few notes on the chart. "I notice she isn't wearing a medic alert tag. Has she been an asthmatic for long?"

Eric nodded. "I guess it depends on what you mean by asthmatic. She has a severe allergy to animals. Her symptoms are usually triggered only if she comes in contact with dogs or cats. She's never even been able to go to a zoo. We don't have any pets in the house and my son has to change clothes and shower after he plays with the neighbor's dog, so I really don't understand what happened to her today. Isn't there some test you can do to find out what started it?"

More scribbles on her chart. "Well that sort of sheds a new light on the problem. Let me see what I can find out for you. For the next couple of days she will be getting antibiotics, breathing treatments and some extra oxygen to get this settled down."

"Can I see her yet?" Eric asked.

The intern gave him an odd look. "Mr. Thomas, Robbie Thomas is your son isn't he?"

Eric nodded.

"Well Mr. Thomas Robbie's vital signs are stable but there are other concerns. "

No reaction. "We are puzzled by his present condition. Has your son ever had a seizure or lapsed into a catatonic state?"

When Eric said nothing, the intern touched his arm and asked the same question.

Eric's mind had retreated to another time another place. Yes Robbie had gone into a semi-comatose state on one other occasion. He remained that way until after his mother was buried. Images he never hoped to see again rose in his mind like ghosts in a bottle. He swayed on his feet. The next thing he saw was a glass of water being lifted to his mouth. The intern and a nurse were standing over him. He was seated in a chair in the same waiting room, feeling disoriented. He sipped the proffered water.

He got to his feet. "You'll keep the boy then?" He asked. "Yes of course you'll keep the boy doctor uh....?"

"Oh, I'm sorry Mr. Thomas; I am Dr. Archer, the on call physician. Your little family will be in my care tonight." He didn't seem to hear him.

Dr. Archer and the nurse watched in astonishment as Eric walked out of the hospital without a backward glance.

He walked for three blocks before he hailed a cab, but he didn't go home. He gave the driver the address of an obscure little shop he had been frequenting for the last several weeks. The shop sold very old very rare books. Most of them dealt with the occult or the unexplained. He had come to know the odd little man who owned the shop quite well. Though Eric had been in the shop many, many times he had never seen another customer. A musical tinkle announced his arrival. The place always smelled like old pickles. He figured it was the smell of the old books.

The shop was dim except for a few rays of sun that shot through the few clean spots on the window. Dust fairies danced in the thin spotlights. As always the shop owner, Mr. Portent was nowhere to be seen. Eric picked up a book, "Untapped Powers of The Mind", and began to skim through it. The old man's voice came from the back room.

"Ah, Eric. Back so soon. Something has happened." It was not a question. He came into the room with a small brown volume in his gnarled hand. "I believe this will help you." He said. "When you have read it come back to see me."

Eric looked at the worn cover of the book. It felt warm in his hand. There was no title and as with all the other books he purchased here, there was no price either. When he looked up Mr. Portent was gone. Eric left the customary twenty dollars on the counter as he left.

As Robbie slept he could feel the marmon near him. He sensed the foul odor filling his nostrils. Awake now he was afraid to open his eyes. He could feel the marmon's fetid breath on his face. He wanted to scream but his throat was paralyzed. When something cold touched his face he opened his eyes. The marmon rose on its hind legs, its horrible eyes fixed on Robbie's throat. Saliva dripped from its lips and on to the bed. A black shiny claw lay against his cheek. Robbie looked one last time into the eyes of the marmon. There was no sign of love there now, only an expression of unparalleled hunger. The cold tip of the claw pierced Robbie's cheek. Blood spurted in the marmon's face. White hot pain seared his face as the marmon ripped him open.

The marmon shook him, howling his name. Robbie screamed and screamed and screamed.

"Robbie! Robbie wake up honey. You're having a nightmare. Open your eyes and look at me." Said an unmarmon like voice. He opened his eyes to a pretty nurse in a blue flowered shirt. The shirt was a uniform smock and the girl was an R.N. on the children's floor. At the moment Robbie didn't give a rip what she was as long as she wasn't the marmon! He threw his arms around her neck and hung on for dear life. She stroked the back of his head speaking quietly.

"You were dreaming Robbie. It was just a nightmare and it's all gone now. You're safe in the hospital and your aunt is just down the hall. She's safe too. O.k.?" As she spoke the memory of the dream disappeared.

He couldn't seem to remember anything, even what day it was. He felt as though something terrible had passed close to him but now it was gone away. Robert Sydney Thomas was now nothing more, nothing less than a terrified four year old boy getting over a really bad dream.

The nurse untied his soaked gown and pulled it off from him. "I'll be right back. I'm just going for a clean gown." She said. "I promise I'll come right back." And true to her word she was back, clean gown in hand in less than three minutes. Robbie couldn't remember what the dream was about. All he knew for sure is that he wanted his dad and his aunt Suz to take him home where he would be safe.

Eric sat at his desk staring at the little brown book from Mr. Portent's shop. His desk was littered with such books. Why would this one be any more likely to give him the answers he so desperately needed than the others had. None of the books from Portent's shop bore the name of a publisher, a copyright or a title. All of them had given him some information but none were conclusive enough to provide an absolute remedy. Still he felt he was on the right track. If it were possible to drive out the evil that had entered their lives, he would not rest until he discovered how it could be done.

He started this journey by delving into children's imaginary friends. They were very common but almost always benign in nature. He read about poltergeists, evil spirits, witches, conjurers, spells and incantations. He even read about pookas, mischievous Irish spirits like the one in the movie,

Harvey. He read about telekinesis, and other powers of the mind. Nothing had jumped out at him that would shed much light on his suspicions about his son. But as he opened the little brown book with the warm cover he found himself transported to a time and place of myth and fantasy made fact.

The author of this book, whose anonymity would forever remain intact, seemed to be speaking directly to Eric about Robbie. The words flew off the pages into his heart and mind, making him see, making him understand. It seemed only seconds passed but Eric was on the last page. A hand written footnote glared up at him. It read. *"Now you are ready to come and see me Eric."*

Eric checked his watch. He had been sitting here reading for four hours. It was after eleven o'clock at night. Every shop in town would be closed but somehow he knew Mr. Portent would be waiting for him. There he knew he would find the answers to his past and the hope for his future. He also felt an urgency quicken his heartbeat. Time was running out. And suddenly he understood what was driving him so hard. He was close to ending this horror and "The Bad Thing", as Robbie called it, knew it too.

In a place unseen by man, the metamorphosis was complete. All that was evil had been cleansed from the boy to feed the thing that had once been the marmon. Now in its pure and undefiled state, the soul of the child waited, unprotected, for the bad thing to come.

Driven by hunger and rage the marmon felt a new urgency. It sensed another was coming, would try to enter it's realm with but a single purpose, to steal its reason for being. The insatiable thing that had once

been the marmon felt a ripple of fear. It must hasten
to finish the task for which it had been prepared.

Mr. Portent rose from his chair when Eric arrived. His
ancient eyes searched Eric's face.

"You already know what it is that stalks your family.
You already know how to defeat it. You have always
known Eric."

Eric shook his head. "But I don't know Mr. Portent.
There is something missing. You know what it is, I
can feel it. Please help me. Please." He pleaded.

The old man reached inside his jacket and brought
out a small object. He held it out to Eric The tiny thing
in the palm of his hand looked much like a mouse or a
shrew, except that its fur was a vibrant red in color.

"What is it Mr. Portent?" He whispered.

"You know what it is Eric. After all, you once had one exactly like it. Go ahead, touch it."

When Eric hesitated, Mr. Portent thrust it at him.

Reluctantly Eric touched the tiny creature. At once the room was filled with tendrils of blue light. The old man straightened to his full height. Except for his eyes, he no longer looked old. His skin seemed to glow in the circle of spectral light. Outside the circle the room began to fade. Suddenly Marie was with them. She was more beautiful than ever. He reached out to touch her face but she shook her head. She beckoned him to look above the circle. As he did so a scene from the past unfolded there. Marie was in the delivery room, giving birth to a tiny red faced baby boy. She was crying tears of joy. He found himself smiling at a moment in time when everything was right and good.

Portent's voice rang in his head. "Yes Eric, it was truly perfect. There was still time then to stop the bad thing from entering this new life."

Eric shook his head. What was he talking about? What bad thing? But even as his thoughts formed, a cold, sad truth was rising from his innermost memories. These were the memories he was sure had died long ago. He took great care to bury them deep. Time shifted. Marie stood in the nursery rocking a two month old Robbie. He was crying, his little fists balled up, his face scrunched up and red.

Eric watched himself stroll into the room with a frown on his face. He heard the impatience in his voice. "Marie we have to go now, we're already late. Put him in the crib. The sitter's here, he'll be fine. Let's go!"

The minute she put him down he started to howl. Eric shook his head. "Can't we get anywhere on time anymore?" He crossed the room to the crib. "You go on and dress, I'll stay with him while you get ready."

Marie looked unsure but did as he asked.

Within the blue circle Eric tried to look away but Marie spoke in his mind. "You must watch Eric, you must remember."

He watched himself take the baby from the crib to rock him gently. The baby only screamed louder. For only an instant Eric felt the heat of hatred touch his soul. The baby had taken priority over every aspect of their lives. Marie's every waking moment was devoted to Robbie. Eric felt like an outsider in his own home. He held the baby closer, chastising himself for his selfishness. He cooed at the little baby in his arms and felt better. Robbie sensed his father's feelings and quieted.

He put the sleepy baby in the crib, brushing a kiss on his downy head. He felt guilty as he left the nursery. These awful feelings of jealousy and hatred were becoming more prevalent than his feeling of love for his son. Where was this coming from? He'd seen many of his friends with their newborns. They were so happy and contented. Somehow his instincts were flawed. Regrettably Eric saw his son as an intruder, an inconvenience.

That seed would take root and grow inside the man and eventually in the child.

Reflections of other times swam into his circle. He saw flashes of anger at the child for the most minor things. As the little boy grew there were times when he barely maintained control. Robbie's room was strewn with toys, he couldn't eat or drink anything without making a major mess of himself, and he was continually whining about something. What was worse, Marie always took Robbie's side, and when she did, Robbie took great pleasure in staying just out of her sight so he could give Eric a triumphant smirk. It was then that Eric realized he was beginning to hate his own son.

Again he tried to look away, but she entreated him to watch and remember. With a sinking heart he watched the months and years speed by. And the bad thing grew between them. He saw himself sitting on Robbie's bed when he was almost four years old. He had been crying. His eyes were filled with loathing as he stared at his father. The very air seemed to crackle between them. The fight was the same one they had at least once a month for the past year. Robbie wanted a pet.

He wheedled and whined all through dinner that evening. It was made worse because Marie's sister was visiting for the weekend. She left that night, thinking she was partly responsible for the rift.

Eric was beyond patience with Robbie tonight. He had ruined dinner, driven his aunt Suzan out of the house and made Marie miserable with the constant bickering between them.

"You will not be getting a pet Robbie. Not a dog, or a cat or even a pet spider. You've made your aunt Suzan feel bad because she thinks it's her fault that you're being deprived of having a pet. It isn't just her allergies that helped me make this decision; it's the sneaky way you do things behind my back. You're always trying to turn your mother against me. So here's the deal, I'm going to tell you about the pet I had when I was a kid, a pet I'm going to give to you with my blessing. And I promise you that it will be the only pet you will ever have."

Eric listened in horror as he heard himself tell his little boy about the pet that came to live with him. He put his hands over his ears but the voice was in his mind and would not be shut out.

"When I was a little boy I lived with a man who beat me and locked me in a closet because he hated me. I couldn't get away from this man because he was my father.

One day a stray dog came in to our yard. The dog and I played all day till my father got home. I took a chance and asked my father if I could keep it. He took me by the arm and showed me what happened to animals that strayed onto our farm. He made me watch while he loaded his shotgun and shot the dog in the head. Then he made me bury it out behind the barn.

I cried more tears that day than I cried the whole of my life. My father talked to me while he watched me dig the hole."

Eric repeated his father's words to his wide eyed little son, each like a hammer blow to his heart.

"He told me that if I wanted a pet of my own, he had the perfect one for me. He told me it was invisible to everyone else, but I would see it as a little, red, furry friend. He said this was a perfect pet for a wicked, useless boy. Then he told me that if I was a bad boy, this thing, would begin to grow because it ate the bad parts of little boys and eventually it would eat my soul. And when it came, just as he said it would, it was just a pet until it ate all the bad feelings I had and grew bigger and stronger each time I did something I wasn't supposed to. It grew big and terrible Robbie and it scared me so bad that I screamed in my room every night when it came. I'm giving it to you Robbie.

If you behave yourself it will be small and friendly. But if you're not a good boy it will come to eat all that bad you make. Then it will grow into a monster. Do you understand what I'm telling you Robbie?"

The little boy on the bed was quiet. Eric thought he had probably gone too far, but the expression in his son's eyes rekindled his anger. Robbie wasn't in the least bit frightened. He remained defiant. The war wasn't over. Eric barely kept himself from slapping that arrogant face.

As he watched the scene play itself out he saw himself storm out of the room. He watched as his son's chin began to quiver, and his eyes tearing up. How could he have been so cruel? He felt a tear slide down his own cheek. Then something he had not seen on that night a year ago caught his eye. Something on the end of Robbie's bed.

Eric choked out the words; "The Marmon!"

He watched as Robbie wiggled his feet closer to the marmon. In horror he listened to his son talking to it.

"Dad doesn't know that I already had you. He thinks he gave you to me. He must be stupid. Only me and you know that I wished you here. And boy is he ever stupid if he thinks you would ever hurt me or be mean. He doesn't know nothing. And I hate him."

Echoing from the past the words came at him, the same words he had said to the marmon when he was a child. In a heartbeat it all came rushing back. His childhood, his father, and their malignant relationship and worst of all the marmon and what it would become.

He found himself sitting on the floor with his hands over his eyes. Marie was gone, only Portent remained.

"It was your father who first opened the door to an unspeakable evil Eric... He conjured it from the hatred he had for the world in which he lived but especially for the hatred he had for you. And as your father gave it to you, so you gave it to your own son. "

Eric poured his torment out in sobs of anguish as Portent continued. "You were spared from things that your son was not weren't you? The evil that grew within you, the evil that fed the marmon was turned back by the sacrifice your mother made. Open your mind Eric. Open your heart and remember." The tiny marmon in his hand whined softly. The room disappeared.

Slowly he became aware of a child sobbing. Above him a room appeared. A small boy, whom Eric recognized as himself was tied to a support beam in the middle of that room. A mixture of hatred and fear shown on the boy's face as he stared at the man standing in front of him. The man was Eric's father. In his hand he held a strap. The cruel pleasure he took in beating the boy shown on his face.

"You think you can get away with threatening to kill me boy?" He screamed. "You're gonna kill me and feed me to your pet huh? Your pet marmon. You really dumb enough to believe there is a marmon you fool? You're too stupid to figure out I made all that stuff up ain't you? Well there ain't no marmon. There ain't nothing in this world gonna keep me from peeling the hide off you tonight boy, right down to the bone. I'll teach you who runs this place and it ain't you or your worthless mother neither."

He cracked the strap. It sounded like a gunshot in the empty shed.

"When I get done with you, you'll wish it was the marmon that had ya stead of me. You payin' attention to me boy?"

But Eric was looking over his father's shoulder where a twelve foot, long toothed animal drooled onto itself as it watched with its three yellow eyes.

Each time the strap bit into him the marmon squealed with delight. It became more repugnant with each blow. Eric thought one more strike would kill him for sure. But as his father drew back his arm to finish him, a sound that he would never forget filled his head. It was the sound of splintered bone and gushing blood. It was the sound and the smell of a tire iron descending on his father's head, again and again. The avenging angel wielding the instrument of death was his mother. She did the only thing she could to save her son.

A roar of anguish filled every corner of the shed. The marmon was cheated of it's reward. A single act of purest love from a mother to her son sent it back to the hell from whence it came.

"Your mother perished that same night when her heart gave out. She paid the ultimate price to save you. But she didn't kill the marmon Eric. You kept it alive with your hatred for your father. Evil and hatred go hand in glove Eric. Your mother's love for you kept the marmon from consuming you. Robbie did not have that protection. His mother was taken from him too early by an already powerful entity that you allowed back into this world and into your son's life. When she died you would not allow yourself to remember the very thing that destroyed Marie and now threatens to destroy what is left of your son. You have allowed this evil to live and to grow. Marie died because the marmon used the anger in Robbie to become strong enough to remove the formidable obstacle of her love." He watched Eric fight the demons of memory.

"You remember now don't you? You heard Marie trying to soothe Robbie's hurt feelings. You heard him lash out at her, accusing her of loving you and hating him. You lost your temper then and hit him several times before Marie could stop you. It was you who fed the marmon with your anger and hatred that night. It was you who made it strong enough to take her life."

Eric shook his head, a sob escaped him. He didn't want to hear anymore, couldn't bear to hear another word. "Please God! Let it end!" But there was more that Portent had to say.

"It is only you that can stop the marmon from finally claiming the thing it came into this world to get Eric. The thing it was denied all those years ago because of your mother's sacrifice, the soul of an innocent, a soul made pure by relinquishing it's evil to something that could survive it, which would thrive on it. The soul it seeks is your sons' and it is you who can stop it."

He felt as though the breath had been knocked out of him. It was all true. Everything that had happened to Marie, to Suzan and to Robbie was because of the evil spawned of the hatred he and his father shared. Hatred so malignant that it's result was the inception of the marmon.

"I don't know how. It's too strong!" He sobbed. "How can I hope to kill it?"

"The answer lies within you Eric. It rests with the love you bear your wife and son."

"But I have never loved my son. You said so yourself."

"No Eric, I didn't say you don't love your son, I said you would not allow yourself to love your son. You have always loved Robbie but you buried that love. Your father's influence and that of the slumbering marmon he created kept you from realizing the truth. Marie never doubted it, and now you know it too."

Truth comes in stealth but warms the soul and strengthens with its dawning. He took Portent's hand and pulled himself to his feet. Portent held the marmon out to Eric. It purred softly.

"This marmon is pure, untainted by evil. It has not been brought into this world by anyone. It has been sent for you. It is the embodiment of innocence, courage and love. It is given to you and your son. Take it."

Eric left the shop running. He didn't look back. The little marmon purred quietly in his pocket.

With a sigh of contentment Mr. Portent, his shop and all his books vanished before   Eric could hail a cab. Many generations of Thomas's would live and die before he would be needed again.

Suzan was drowning. Desperately she tried to pull herself up, fighting for one gulp of life giving air. She could see light above. Just a little further now. An explosion of light and sound engulfed her as she broke the surface. Gasping and coughing she pushed at the hands trying to push her back down. "No, no..." She begged. Another great lung full of air and her hands flew to her face. She was being smothered by something over her mouth. Her eyes focused on the face of a young man. On her mouth was an oxygen mask. The young man with the anxious look on his face was dressed all in white.

"Am I dead?" She heard herself croak. He took the mask off.

"Far from it Suzan. You are in the hospital. You were in severe respiratory distress when you came in. You're going to be just fine. In fact we think we've found what it was that triggered the attack. Your little nephew was brought in with you." Suzan sat up alarmed. "No need to worry, just a mild case of shock. Seems he actually called 911 to get help. He must have had a panic attack when you went into respiratory arrest. He was unconscious when the paramedics got there. Trust me though he really is fine. But getting back to your respiratory problem, when we were undressing your nephew we found some long black hairs in his pocket. Your brother in law told us you don't have any pets because of your allergies so we figure your nephew must have been playing with one hellacious big dog in the neighborhood and ended up with several of the animals hairs in his pocket. They very probably caused your difficulties."

"Are you taking care of Robbie too?" Suzan asked.

"Yes, I am Dr. Archer. I was the physician on call when you both came in. We got rid of the animal hairs we found in Robbie's clothes. If I were you I would make sure he stays away from the dog. Aside from the fact that you are highly allergic reaction this dog seems to have rolled in some carrion. The odor was horrible."

"Yes I will talk to him about it. I'm surprised he didn't mention a new dog in the neighborhood. He always tells us about the other children's pets. I feel very bad about being the cause of his not being allowed to have one of his own." She finished miserably.

Doctor Archer patted her hand. "I'm sure that Robbie thinks his lovely aunt Suzan is much more important to him than a dog." He smiled.

Suzan felt herself blushing furiously.

"I'll look in on you in a little while Suzan. Get some rest."

When he left the room she thought about what he had said about Robbie saving her life. He had called 911. She should be proud and grateful to him but something didn't feel right. She closed her eyes trying to remember. She left her room this morning and ran in to Robbie with an armload of bedding but after that things got a bit vague. She fell asleep seeing Robbie's terrified face swimming above her.

Eric tip toed to her bedside and brushed a kiss on her forehead. He was happy not to see the oxygen mask covering her face. It was very late, almost morning by now. Robbie was on the floor above in the pediatric wing. He hurried to the elevator. He was relieved no one was around. He didn't want to take the time to try and explain why he had to be here at this hour with his son.

The elevator seemed to crawl slowly upward. He prayed that he would know what to do when the time came. "I have to stop the marmon from reaching my son." He murmured.

The elevator stopped. The little marmon in his pocket wiggled. Eric knew this little creature was the key. "God help me finish this." He prayed. The elevator doors didn't open. Seconds ticked by. He pushed the "open door" button. Nothing happened.

Panicky now he tried to pry the doors open. He got a small opening and peered through the crack. The elevator had stopped mid floor. He swore silently. He knew this was the marmon trying to keep him away. The little marmon began to whine. Time was running out. Frantic, he pounded on the doors. Someone was sure to hear him. No one did. The emergency phone was dead. He knew it would be. Suddenly the elevator moved a few inches. The doors opened. He could see the sign in the hallway. This was the pediatric ward. He pulled himself up through the half opened doors. He jumped clear just as the elevator doors slammed shut.

He stood there shaking as the unmistakable screech of a falling elevator gave way to the terrible sound of the elevator impacting the basement floor. The blood drained from his face. Just a millisecond more and he would have either been cut in half by the closing doors or become a mound of flesh mixed with the debris in the basement.

He sprinted for his son's room. The odor hit him before he opened the door. It smelled of putrefying flesh. He gagged as he pushed through the door. The room was dark. He felt along the wall for the light switch. It didn't work. He stood stark still listening. He heard raspy breathing across the room. The sound of something scraping the floor came from the same vicinity.

Terror gripped him. Was he too late? Softly he called out.

"Robbie can you hear me? It's dad. Please answer me Robbie." He pleaded.

He tried to hear past the sounds of the marmon for his son's breathing. He wasn't sure what he heard until…

"He… isss… mine…" The marmon had his son!

Each hair on the back of Eric Thomas's head stood at full attention. His blood felt like ice water in his veins. A small whimper came from his pocket. Eric shoved his hand in. The warm little animal clutched at his fingers. The warmth turned to heat, then to fire. His hand was burning. He tried to pull his hand free but the tiny marmon held him fast. He grit his teeth with the pain. A soft glow of blue light outlined the shape of the monster looming over his son. Luminous yellow eyes turned their attention to Eric. And suddenly he knew what he had to do. His hand came easily from his pocket. As he did so blue sparks danced along his fingers.

The little marmon was gone. Tendrils of blue flame shot from his hand. The monster screamed as the flames scored its fur and into its flesh. Another flame shot out hitting it in one of its yellow eyes. It bellowed in rage. Screaming and frothing it advanced on Eric. The flame in his hand now filled him with a growing power. He glanced at his son lying on the bed. There bathed in blue light was his Marie. Both were smiling at him. He smiled at them. A feeling of infinite peace and love enveloped him. And suddenly he understood it all.

He met the marmon in the middle of the room. There he stretched out his arms taking the marmon in his embrace. It struggled against him. Outrage poured from its throat as it fought to escape. Wraithlike coils of fire engulfed man and beast as they grappled there. A sigh from the man, a last cry of disbelief from the beast as the flames rose to consume them entirely.

It was Doctor Archer who found Eric's lifeless body lying at the foot of his son's bed the next morning. He rang for the duty nurse who upon entering immediately burst into tears. Robbie sat next to his father's body with a look of such tenderness on his face that it nearly broke her heart.

Doctor Archer gathered the boy in his arms and went to Suzan's room. She was devastated when he told her that Eric had died of an apparent coronary sometime in the night. Together she and Robbie wept their hearts out. Robbie was now an orphan. There was only he and aunt Suzan now.

When they went home it was to stay. Eric and Marie left everything to Suzan and Robbie. It was almost a year before the weight of their grief became bearable enough for them to resume their lives. Suzan went back to teaching when Robbie started first grade. They found a routine in their lives once more and eventually peace.

Two years later, thanks to Doctor Archer and his diligent research, Robbie was able finally to have his very own puppy. Suzan didn't mind the shots she had to have monthly one little bit. Watching Robbie and his puppy playing in the yard or roughhousing inside made it well worth the little sting of a needle once a month.

The year after that Doctor Archer married Suzan and adopted Robbie. They were the epitome of the American dream in their circle. They were a well respected, well liked family in the community. Eric and

Marie could rest in peace seeing the happiness they helped foster.

Every once in a while Robbie would wake from a nightmare he couldn't remember. It was on these nights that he was especially glad that he wasn't alone. His dog snored softly on the floor beside his bed. He leaned over to scratch behind his long ears. The dog stretched himself and rolled onto his back.

Robbie wiggled his toes in the silky warmth of his other friend at the foot of his bed. His little red belly rose and fell as he slept. How lucky could a boy be to have two pets to love him?

My Grandma's Apron

"You're just like your grandmother."

If I'd heard it once I heard it a thousand times. It was only as I approached womanhood that I began to understand and appreciate what that actually meant, or how deep it would grow.

When I was a kid I remember watching my grandmother cooking in her antiquated kitchen. She had a pump in the sink, and a giant black wood stove that took small to medium sized pieces of wood to fuel the heat. How she managed to figure out how and when the temperature was right was a mystery.

To say she was an excellent cook would be the understatement of the century. She was nothing short of magical, and I mean that in more than one way.

My mother and father were killed in a horrendous tornado that destroyed most of the little town of Hamlin when I was three years old. I happened to be spending the weekend with my grandparents when it happened and I never left the farm after that.

I couldn't remember much about them so I didn't miss them much. Life on the farm was so warm and peaceful; I never had time to reflect on their absence. I had no other relatives except my grandparents and they were my world.

When I was big enough to kneel on a kitchen chair and reach the table, grandma presented me with a miniature duplicate of the full apron she wore when she cooked.

From the moment the soft fragrant cloth touched my skin I was filled with new thoughts and feelings. I was so happy and proud. I had a confidence I never had before. I know it sounds crazy but some sort of instinct took over and my hands began to act of their own accord.

Ingredients filled the bowls as beautiful creations in pastries and breads took form.

Even at my tender age, everything that we made together was superb. It never occurred to me to wonder how the flour and other ingredients suddenly became the right consistency to make anything I wanted, cakes, biscuits, pies, rolls, anything I wanted.

Grandpa would wink his eye at me as he sank his teeth into a piece of pie and say, "You're just like your grandmother." He'd chuckle.

She would smile at him with that special twinkle of affection they shared. Theirs was a true love story.

Grandma told me never to let anyone else touch my apron, ever. When we were finished with our baking she took her apron and mine to the pantry and put them in a special chest, she called the magic box.

As I grew up our baked goods had become a cottage industry in the area. People came from counties away just to buy what we made. Oh it wasn't just the taste and texture of the goods. People said that they felt better not just physically but in other ways as well, often remarking that they were so comforted when they were enjoying something we made. Others said they were finding a wonderful contentment they hadn't known.

Our little corner of the world did seem to enjoy the lowest crime rate in the state. We were a community of friends and neighbors, even though many miles separated most of us, like most farming communities.

While I was growing up, the bus came everyday to take me the twenty two miles to Hamlin, until I graduated at seventeen. I had many friends as a teenager but not many of them were interested in spending time on my grandparent's farm but there were always visitors at the farm. From the early morning breads, to the afternoon rolls and pastries, someone was always stopping in to buy them.

Those who were our nearest neighbors and regular customers were always saying that I was just like my grandmother. I was pleased that they thought so. She was a gentle little lady with a quick wit and a high intellect.

When the day was done, we would all sit out on the porch listening to the peeping frogs and crickets. It was a perfect existence. Nothing or no one in this world could ever drag me away from this place, this life. I was content.

On my twenty first birthday, Grandpa had a stroke. Grandma and I were preparing a large order for a banquet when we heard him cry out.

We rushed to the bathroom where we found him conscious but unable to talk. His right arm flailed about but it was obvious that his left side was paralyzed.

Grandma rode in the ambulance with grandpa. I followed in grandpa's new pickup truck, scared half out of my wits.

At the hospital the doctors confirmed that it was a stroke but assured us that it was mild and that most of the paralysis could be helped with rehabilitation.

Grandma sent me home after I had a chance to give him a big kiss and hug. He smiled a lopsided goodbye as I left. She reminded me that we had several large orders to fill that afternoon. Then she said a strange thing to me. She whispered in my ear that I should wear her apron just for today. She was very adamant about it so I agreed.

The sight that greeted me in the kitchen was one of chaos. There was spilled flour, bowls turned over, and utensils on the floor. There was even a broken baking dish on the counter. Such was our haste in getting to grandpa.

The size and complexity of the baked goods order was suddenly overwhelming. I sat at the counter with my head in my hands considering calling the customers to apologize and cancel the order. I was sure they would understand under the circumstances.

I decided to take a few moments to clean the mess before I made the call. I went to the pantry and opened the magic box to get an apron. As I stood looking into the empty box, I was baffled. Where were our aprons? I was sure I saw grandma put them in there before she got into the ambulance.

My mind wouldn't register what my eyes were telling me. I reached into the empty box. Ahhhh…

When the last pan of brioche was packed in a box and sealed for pick up, I wiped my hands on my grandmother's apron. A tingle of satisfaction went through me. The order was filled, the kitchen cleaned and everything put away. That is everything but grandma's apron.

I smiled as I dropped the apron in to the empty magic box, knowing that when I opened it again it would be empty. Yep I'm just like my grandmother.

The Fourth Boy

My junior year at Hamlin University was a ball breaker. Working part time to pay for tuition, books and classes coupled with my scholastic workload left me drained. Small wonder that when my roommate brought up the subject of spring break and a possible road trip, that I shook my head no. All I wanted to do for the next two weeks was sleep.

My roommate was never one to give up easily. He painted a picture of sunshine, sandy beaches, cheap booze and wild women. He nagged me about being a dull fellow/wall flower, adding that I was becoming a bore at nineteen years of age. Spring break was still one week away and the weather in Hamlin was still in the thirties with snow flurries forecast for the next five days. The more he talked the better it sounded. He could see I was caving. There would be four of us if I decided to go. I wavered, he pressed. When he knew he had me he hit me with the real reason he so desperately wanted me to go.

They needed a fourth guy to put up the rest of the money for the vacation package they were pushing. By the time they got around to the financial end of it, I was frothing at the mouth to get the hell out of Hamlin and into some warm tropical sun. The babes and booze was just frosting on the cake. As always the dilemma was a severe lack of cash. There was only one place I could even hope to get that much cash, Grandpa. He and I had a very special bond, as my dad was an absentee father. Grandpa always told me if I ever needed anything to let him know. Many times he had offered to help out with my education but I was determined to make my own way. Secretly I think he was proud of me for that.

Sundays were reserved for my visits to Grandpa at the senior living center where he lived. It was like a little city of old people. These old people were not your average cane and walker folks. This geriatric population hiked, played badminton, shuffleboard, and had cook outs, dances, parties. Hell they had more fun and energy than I did! This Sunday they were putting on a Mexican fiesta dinner with tacos, enchiladas, burritos, Spanish rice, you name it they had it. Grandpa met me at the door wearing a huge sombrero and a goofy looking serape over his customary long sleeved plaid shirt. He looked about as Mexican as a cocker spaniel. He was smiling and singing his version of La Cucaracha as he ushered me in the door.

The whole day was a hoot. People were doing the Mexican hat dance and gorging themselves on cuisine that would later take massive quantities of antacid tablets to quell the fire in their bellies. When things wound down I told him I needed to talk to him so he said goodnight to his friends and we walked across the square to his apartment.

As always he asked if I needed anything, and this time I told him I did. I told him about the vacation package the guys were trying to put together, leaving out the babes and booze part, heavy emphasis on the sun, the sea, and the tropical fruit. He listened carefully occasionally nodding his head until I finished with my request for three hundred dollars paying my share of the cost. He rose from his chair without a word and went to his bedroom, returning with not three but five hundred dollars. I told him it was too much but he insisted I take the full amount. As he handed me the money he held on to it for a moment.

He looked me directly in the eyes and said he had something to share with me before I took it. A story, he said, a tale to be considered and to judge as true or fairy tale, but not one to be taken lightly. I sat back in my chair and listened with deepening interest as the narrative unfolded. He began;

That spring break was the bomb! All four of the Hamlin University students were in various stages of consciousness slumped in the seats of the 747 on its flight back to the United States. Four little kings sleeping off the effects of their last night of debauchery out of their parents and U.S. official jurisdiction. Wealthy and without a thought in the world for anyone but themselves, they slept the sleep of the protected.

Five days and four nights of drinking, fornication, and pranking everyone including each other left them exhausted, and anxious to get back to campus. They could hardly wait to brag about the fine time they had, the fine women they had and the colossal alcohol binges they went on. Of course they left out the part about the copious vomiting and gargantuan hangovers. The local scene was too tame, the hotel too mundane for these little monarchs. Oh they drank themselves stupid and picked up a few women they had to pay for, they even did a few base jumps off a cliff they never would have braved sober, but their craving for the ultimate adrenaline rush wasn't even close to being satisfied.

How clever they all thought they were, hiring a luxury boat to explore the remote Islands they had flown over on their way to New Guinea. How lucky they were to find on one of those little known islands a whole tribe of people just waiting to fulfill their every wish. The women were ripe for the taking. No one objected no matter how cruel they were. Age didn't matter either. Some of the women might have been as young as twelve. They spent a day and a night on the island getting their fill of humiliating and debasing the locals. By that time their supply of liquor was nearly exhausted and they were becoming bored.

To add insult to injury they took particular pleasure in the destruction of many wooden statues of lizard like beings on the island. That, however, was not the end of their sordid behavior. Every time they turned over a statue or broke a totem, dozens of tiny lizards scattered in all directions. They spent a good deal of time trying to catch a few of them but they were not quick enough. It was this final insult that caused the natives to become agitated. They put themselves between the animals and the boys, finally threatening them with clubs. It was time to leave.

But for right now they were snug in their little seats, visiting their private little dreamlands unaware of the forces they set in motion when they carried two tiny lizards on board with them. Their plan was to release them once aboard to scare the hell out of the passengers. That plan would never see fruition.

The lizards were on the window sill of two of the boy's room their last morning as they packed to leave the hotel. They were the same kind that the boys had chased on the island. There were four to begin with. Jerry, the oldest and the nastiest of the four boys, smashed two of them with his shoe before the other boy stopped him. It was Dan, the cleverest, and he had a better idea. He dumped his toothbrush out of its holder and put the two remaining lizards inside. He tucked it in his pocket where he figured everyone could see it was just a toothbrush holder.

They didn't even bother to clean up the smashed carcasses of the dead lizards. What the hell their folks had paid big money for the hotel staff to give them the royal treatment they felt they so richly deserved. They left the disheveled room without a backward glance.

An hour later as the hotel cleaning staff was entering that room; the four hellions were just boarding the plane. Five minutes later the native woman cleaning their hotel room found the disemboweled bodies of the discarded lizards. Immediately she felt the little hairs on her arms rise and fall. These little creatures weren't just any reptiles; these were sacred to the natives, most especially to the head of a local island tribe, for it was by the power of these tiny lizard gods of protection that he was made King and kept safe from lesser but more malevolent gods.

With great care she scraped the tiny animals into a cloth, wrapped them up and put them in her bag. A tear of despair rolled down her cheek. There was sadness for the deaths of these two innocents, and hopelessness for the bad people who had taken their lives. She was bound by loyalty and tradition to present herself before the tribal King to make him aware of this sacrilege. She wished she had chosen another room to clean and let someone else make this discovery. As it happened she was now committed to take part in the ceremony that would appease the vengeful appetites of the offended gods. The results would be horrifying.

Quickly she gave the room a light cleaning, not her usual meticulous job. She had to hurry. Neither the tribal King nor the gods would have patience with her if she lingered.

Grandpa paused in his story for a sip of water. By this time I was curious to know who these guys were, if they actually existed, but Grandpa raised a hand before I got a word out. For the next half hour I said nothing. For the half hour after that there was nothing I could say. He continued, speaking quietly and calmly as if he was telling me a bed time story, but believe me this was not a story you would tell a child!

A little turbulence woke clever Dan from his dreams. The plane was dark except for tiny dim lights over each seat. The passengers were all sleeping. He stretched and yawned and remembered the tooth brush holder in his pocket. Snickering he took it from his pocket intending to drop the lizards on the back of the seat in front of him. There were no lizards in the holder. Squirming around in his seat he felt himself from top to bottom in case they were in his clothes. He sighed, no lizards there. They must have gotten out and wandered off while he slept. He grinned. Sooner or later some unsuspecting woman would scream when one of the reptiles climbed her leg or fell in her hair. He decided to get a little more sleep while the lizards chose their mark.

Jerry snored beside him while the other two boys were passed out in the seats across the aisle. There were a number of hours before landing in the United

States and except for the stewardess serving them dinner there wasn't anything else to do. The airline didn't show the kind of movies he liked to watch, too tame.

Jerry opened his eyes. Jerry wiped his eyes. Jerry shook his head. There was something wrong. Slowly he opened his right eye. He looked straight ahead. Everything seemed normal. The seat in front of him was blue and white and upright. Above the back of the seat he could see a white tuft of hair from the old man who occupied it. He felt his heartbeat slowing back to normal. Then, snap! His eye rotated a full hundred and eighty degrees. He sucked air as his eye settled on the seat to his right, across the aisle and two seats back. Such a feat was not possible without turning his head or turning his body in the seat, but he had remained stationary. Yet there was the little

Philippine lady with the purple purse he had passed on the way to his seat when he boarded.

He slammed his eye shut. This was a hallucination. Too much booze, not enough sleep, something in the water. His jaw went slack as darkness took him.

Dan wrinkled his nose in disgust. Jerry must be farting his ass off. Holy crap what a stench! He was about to punch Jerry in the arm when he realized he was inhaling his own body odor. When he moved the smell became stronger. Man oh man, he couldn't smell this rank! He took a shower this morning before they left the hotel. He put a hand to his mouth exhaling into it. He gagged. The smell was enough to back up a truck! He looked around to see if anyone else noticed where the stink was coming from. So far no one had. For two or three seconds he considered going to the restroom to freshen up and brush his teeth. Oh yeah, he had no tooth brush. That was his last thought as he drifted off to fantasy land.

The next conscious thought Dan had was that his arm really hurt. Something had clamped on to it with a flesh piercing grip. He looked down to see Jerry's clawed hand gripping his forearm. He looked into Jerry's eyes and froze. Jerry's mouth was moving, his thin lips trying to form words around a protruding little forked tongue. His face was mottled and grey.

Jerry tried to communicate but only little squeaks came out. He stared at Dan, his eyes pleading for his friend to help him somehow. Then, snap! His eyeballs both shot to their outside orbits on each side of his face. He could clearly see the airplane window on his right with his right eye while his left took in the horrified look on Dan's face. Somewhere in the far reaches of Jerry's mind he sensed a putrid aroma filling his nostrils. He understood somehow that the smell was coming from Dan but coherent thought was fast receding from his mind. Dan reached a scaly hand toward Jerry in an attempt to escape the stranglehold he had on his forearm. The sight of his own leathery flesh brought a scream to his lips but no sound emerged. Genuine terror seized the boys as they stared at one another. They were powerless to cry out, powerless to move, powerless to arrest the inflexible metamorphosis shredding and reassembling their DNA.

Across the aisle the other two boys had awakened, their bodies itching and burning. They had been scratching themselves in their sleep. Alarmed that they had contracted some horrible communicable disease from the island natives, they pulled up their sleeves and opened their shirts expecting to see an angry rash. To their horror, the skin on their arms and on their chests were not rashed but had become grayish green and dappled. In a panic they bolted from their seats to see if Dan and Jerry shared their fate, but Dan and Jerry were not in their seats. Only their clothing and shoes remained where the two had been sitting when the plane left New Guinea.

Oh there was a huge scandal and a major investigation on a national and international scale to find out what had happened to the two boys. Speculations abounded, everything from kidnapping to alien abduction was visited over the years. But the mystery was never solved. The boys had reaped what they sowed as is befitting such a tale.

Grandpa got up from his chair and placed the money in my lap. "Spring break", he said, "should be a time of relaxation and fun. Not a time of cruelty and hatred. I'm sure you understand the moral of the story my boy." He patted my cheek and started for the kitchen.

For a moment I just sat there deciding whether to laugh or be concerned about my grandfather's sanity. Finally I decided to make light of it and go along with his outrageous yarn.

"So grandpa what ever happened to the other two boys?" I asked with a half grin on my face.

Grandpa turned to me and began rolling up his sleeves.

"You see my boy; the other two boys had nothing to do with the killing or abduction of the sacred little lizard creatures. Oh they were a part of a wicked, cruelty to those poor natives, but they stopped short of Dan and Jerry's ruthlessness. Punishment was meted out in accordance with the severity of the offense. Otherwise my dear boy I wouldn't be here and neither would you."

I heard his words through the white noise echoing in my mind as I stared at the reptilian skin on his arms. I have no idea how long we sat in silence across from one another. Hundreds of questions filled my mind as I left his apartment that night. For one, how did he explain his appearance to my grandmother? None of my uncertainties were ever voiced, nor did we ever discuss his spring break again. Grandpa made it plain that the subject was closed indefinitely. I left the money he gave me on his coffee table, told my roommate I couldn't get off work and stayed home that spring break. I understood that what my Grandpa was trying to tell me that night went much deeper than some kid's bad behavior on a vacation. How a person conducts himself in all aspects of life determines what he will become.

But you know after eighty three years of shaping and reshaping my life, I still wonder; what ever happened to the fourth boy?

The Fifth of Death

On **The First Day of Death** he opened his mind for thought. Sight was now a thing barely remembered. Eyes that once gave the delight of dimension and color now lay forever unseeing in the cold shell that lay beneath the freshly turned earth.

Images danced before the essence of what he had become. His mind still conjured faces from the life he no longer possessed as they passed before him, bodiless, soundless specters on a carousel. Twenty eight years of memory taunted the soul that swirled in a vortex of space unfamiliar to the living.

He was startled by the ease of his passing. There was no pain, no fear of the unknown. He marveled that there had been no struggle between life and death, only a moment of calm serenity in this first day of death. One merely paused for a moment in one state and then silently passed into the next.

Life was the real struggle. For twenty of his living years he had known only conflict, his existence one of violence and hatred.

In that early plane of existence he was known as Maxwell Daniel Parent. He didn't know where the name came from. He suspected it had nothing at all to do with his heritage. What an impressive name for such a mousy little boy. His mother must have had a moment of pomposity when she decided what to call him. Even in death he felt her reaching out to him with her greed, her possessive domination. Hatred shimmered in waves around him. Was this hell? Dark memories of his life came as unbidden projections on the dark tapestry about him. Yes this must be hell.

He saw himself at eight years old, a pitifully thin, dirty faced little boy in ragged clothes much too large for his slight frame.

The first eight years of his life Max was smothered in his mother's possessiveness. Having nothing to compare it to, he thought it was a perfectly normal and loving mother/son relationship.

There was no reason to question the odd way they lived, he didn't know anything else.

He couldn't miss what he'd never had or couldn't remember. To Max her wildly obsessive behavior was perfectly normal. He was content to spend his days in quiet obedience to his mother's wishes and counted himself lucky to be so loved.

He stayed alone during the nights his mother worked as a waitress in a small diner. He had no friends, was home schooled, and there were no close neighbors to worry about.

Three or four times a month his mother would come reeling into the house in the middle of the night with a man in tow. She introduced them as "uncles". It was never the same man twice, but always the same type. They were all drunk and loud.

He pulled the covers over his head to drown out the sound, knowing that soon she would come in to the bedroom and send him out to sleep on the living room couch. She had other uses for the bed she usually shared with him. In the morning the uncle would usually be gone, sometimes helping themselves to the tip money in his mother's purse on their way out. This same woman held him close to her when she had no other company in her bed. Max felt cherished and safe on those nights.

His mother's male friends came less frequently in the next few months and soon it became apparent why. Things were about to get even stranger.

It was about this time that "daddy Jim" entered their lives. He started showing up on a regular basis, and in a few short weeks he moved in permanently. He looked as big as a mountain to Max. He always wore a nasty smirk and rarely ever spoke without shouting. His mother insisted that he call him, "daddy Jim", and wasn't it wonderful to have a real daddy? Max was terrified.

One night when his mother was gone Max learned a new kind of fear. Daddy Jim came staggering into the living room where Max slept on the couch. It took only seconds for Max to figure out that this huge tub of lard liked little boys just as much as he liked grown up ladies. The fat man was slow and clumsy while Max was young and quick. He escaped his lecherous attentions and fled to the shrubs in the front yard to wait for his mother.

When she pulled in to the drive way he ran as fast as he could to catch her before she got into the house. He threw himself at her, hugging her knees and sobbing. This was where little boys found safety. She would throw the man out.

Sobbing and snorting with frequent swipes to his nose, he poured out his story. He expected her to take him in her arms and comfort him, promising that the man would have to leave. Instead she drew back her arm and slapped him full in the face. She grabbed his arm and slapped him again.

She bent close to his face and through clenched teeth explained to him how things would be.

"I've worked and sweat my ass off for you, you worthless little piece of meat. Now that I finally got a chance to have a man of my own I'm not going to let you screw it up! I've sacrificed my whole life for you but now it's my turn. You hear me? If I ever hear such filthy lies come out of your mouth again I'll turn your ass out on the street like I should a done the day you were born. You understand me?"

She gave him a few shakes for emphasis. She shoved him away as if the very sight of him was repugnant to her. He watched her back as she mounted the steps and disappeared into the house. His legs gave under him. He sat down hard. This couldn't be the same woman who protected him insisting he stay behind locked doors when she wasn't home.

A great sadness washed over him. Darkness and cold finally overcame his fear. His mother was home. He didn't think she would let the man actually hurt him. He would have to find ways to protect himself when she was away.

The following day his mother announced that she would be working the day shift from now on. Max was elated. Days weren't half as scary as night. At first it was easy to avoid the man. As soon as his mother left for work Max grabbed whatever he could find to eat and left the house returning only when her shift was over.

Most of the time the adults ignored him. He had become the invisible boy. He didn't mind at all. They fell into a routine. She would fix dinner; they would drink too much and stagger off to the bedroom. He would clean up the mess and wait for them to fall asleep. Only then did he rest. The end came when his mother left early one morning without telling him. He woke up with a monster looming over him. Paralyzed with fear he shut his eyes. This had to be a nightmare. The monster would go away, but instead a huge hand touched his leg. The hand caressed and slid higher.

Something in Max snapped. A rage was born in him that transcended conscious thought. It wasn't until he stopped screaming that he realized the monster was indeed gone. His body was wet and slippery with the blood of the monster. In his hand he held the old rusty knife he kept under his pillow. His eyes followed the crimson river dripping from his hand. The drops of blood formed a pattern beside the great lump of flesh on the floor. The monster was dead but the rage remained.

He knelt beside the silent hulk on the floor. Methodically he began slicing through flesh and removing parts. The testicles were first, then the penis. He pried open its mouth and stuffed the severed appendages in as far as they would go.

There. Now he could think. And with those thoughts was born a fiery hatred for his mother that would become the driving force for the remainder of his life.

At eight years old he was out on the street, running from the law, and running from her. He never again referred to her as his mother. She had become the "old bitch!"

A little boy's cry echoed in the matrix, frightened and filled with loathing.

"Bitch! Bitch! Old Bitch!"

On the **Second Day of Death**, his mind raced through the years of fear and loneliness. Like a stray dog he wandered the streets, begging for food, stealing when necessary. He slept in doorways, under porches, in alleys behind garbage cans. A shudder passed through the matrix as the memory of a dark night trapped behind the walls of the city zoo floated by. Terror, born anew, eddied and rippled through the dark womb of his present state as he heard again the snarls and howling of animals he could not see.

He became a toughened survivor.

By the time he was thirteen years old hunger and fear had provided all the incentive he needed to become an accomplished thief. If the situation called for him to rough someone up he didn't let that slow him down. In fact he rather enjoyed inflicting pain during the course of picking a pocket or stealing a purse.

At fourteen he added home invasion to his repertoire. There was always a chance someone would be there, someone he could abuse in some way.

As he grew, so grew the flame of his cruelty fueled by his hatred for the bitch that spawned him.

He stole his first car when he was 15. He didn't know how to drive, but the resultant crash did nothing to lessen the rush he got from it, especially the part where he threw the owner out on to the expressway at seventy five miles per hour. He practically drooled when the first car hit the man.

Like finds like and soon he was running with a pack of thrill junkies just like him. Life was good, but somehow the high was never high enough. He needed more.

Max masterminded a bank robbery. He thought he had it all worked out, but, he hadn't taken into consideration that at least half of the scum bags he ran with had lower I.Q.'s than a sea slug. When it was over Max had two revelations; Revelation number one: **Never trust anyone but yourself**. The two guys who entered the bank with him were so high on crack; they couldn't make the clerk understand what they wanted. When Max took over and got the money from the terrified clerk, scum bag number one shot scum bag number two in the foot and alarms started blaring all over the bank.

Trying to get out the door, they banged in to one another and dropped most of the money bags in the doorway.

Speeding down the highway, thinking they got away clean, the car began to spit and sputter, rolling to a gentle stop at the curb. The gas gauge read Empty!

Max took the gun out of his belt and shot the scum bags once each in the middle of the forehead.

Revelation number two: **Killing just to kill was the final and <u>ultimate</u> high**. Killing in self defense couldn't hold a candle to this. Watching the life fade from their eyes, and knowing that he had the power to take it from them was a rush like nothing he'd ever experienced. There was nothing on earth to equal this. Not a pang of regret. No conscience. A murder hungry killer is born.

His reputation grew with his savagery which opened new doors. Underworld crime figures employed his well honed skills. In time even they were astonished at the pleasure he took in torturing his victims, especially middle aged women. He screamed in their faces as he brutalized them. "Bitch! Bitch! Old Bitch!

Not once in his twenty year career did he consider that he would be killed. But the very people who used him also feared him. When that fear was ripe enough death came in the form of a nine millimeter bullet through his brain as he lay in his bed sleeping.

As the bullet penetrated the core of his brain his last and only conscious thought was of his mother. He carried in to death the hatred be bore her in life.

Granted to Max on the **Third Day of Death**, was the power to discern day from night. In the blackness of nowhere and nothing he understood that three days had passed since his death. As darkness receded a keen sense of sorrow filled his being. Alien emotions washed over him. Guilt and fear took possession of him, gnawed at him, and tore through him in twisted waves of agony bringing him to the zenith of abject terror!

A primal shriek incarnate exploded into his placental asylum. The dawning of a new understanding penetrated his consciousness. The empty chasm reacted to the roar of truth grappling with denial.

Something cold stirs inside him. Dark misery flows in little waves filling him. Sorrow as absolute as white sound overwhelms, holds him helpless. All that he ever felt, all that he ever knew is wrung from him. Meaningless and empty, he is a finished absence, an aperture of black loss.

Eddies and currents of something unknown and unwelcome worry at him. A devastating grief begins to grow from the core of him, overpowers and possesses him. Desperate he tries to flee from this new torment. He cries out, but there is no sound here Max. There are no tears from this state of death without voice.

The apex of mourning ripens to a new plateau. And yet something more, something alien to him. He cannot recognize it for what it is. It slithers over him.

No Max, you cannot scream! The faces of his

victims, their cries for mercy, their consummate pain

slams into him with violence inconceivable to him

until this moment. Absolute understanding dawns

within the nucleus of his mind……. Payment is

expected.

With **The Fourth Day of Death** came the infinite

knowledge possessed only by the dead. No

speculation, no acceptance or denial, only a quiet

resignation, a submission to what will come. No

altering that which has already been consummated.

Tomorrow is an accomplished body of facts vividly

projected in that dark pool of time infinite. Perfect

acceptance of the hell designed specifically for him

sends him spiraling over the edge. A dimming echo

follows him down into the unknowable. It is his

mother's voice. "To Hell with you Max!"

On **The Fifth Day of Death** the essence of Maxwell Daniel Parent began the transformation to what he would become. Dimly aware that a change was taking place, he felt himself grow vague. Memory left him. All thought ceased. His consciousness faded, winked out. The abyss, the whole of the great void, black emptiness becomes everything, is all.

Time begins anew. Perpetual evolution of the spirit. Immortal metamorphosis of that which is called 'soul'.

From the matrix of all living things an image of understanding makes the transition from the **Fifth of Death** to the **First day of life**. The inception of animate existence becomes aware. Substance forms dimension. Impressions become instincts. Urgency begins to grow, to ripen, transcending all that went before. Limbs stretch forth. Lungs strain to take in the first sweet breath of life..............

A new being is born.

The birth was an exhausting one for mother and baby. The air felt cool against his wet body, coaxing him to edge closer to his mother. Instinctively he began to push his way into her thick warm fur, searching. Mother began to lick the new born, cleaning the effects of birth from his tiny body as he suckles. There are other sounds here. The timber of voices from somewhere above him send a tremor through his chilled body. The words mean nothing to him. Meaningless noises, yet something about them tugs at him. But now he is sleepy and his tummy is filled from his mother's generous gift. Contented he snuggles closer to *the Old Bitch* that is his mother........

Above him a little girl is watching the puppy sleeping and contented next to the old dog. She is tired of the old dog. It was no fun to play with her anymore.

She claps her hands with the joy of the very young and squeals with delight. She tells her daddy how thrilled she is to have a new puppy. Daddy smiles at his darling little Nancy. She is his world, he denies her nothing. He kisses the top of her adorable head and goes out to clean up after assisting with the birth. Little Nancy smiles him out of the room and turns her attention to the newborn puppy.

The expression in her eyes as she lowers her head to the sleeping puppies' ear is one of gleeful anticipation. She whispers softly to the tiny life sleeping there, "You're mine now, all mine, my very own. I think I'm going to call you Max!"

The tired old dog lifts her head to stare into the cold eyes of the child she has come to hate. A low growl rumbles up from deep inside her. Max would indeed be Nancy's very own. He would take her place now. It would now fall to him to become the beneficiary of

the child's perverse cruelties. ***The Old Bitch***
groaned at the remembered beatings in this very
basement, her mouth taped shut, whimpering into
the darkness, Nancy's laughter ringing in her ears.
Great pain and prolonged hunger had taken their
toll. Too old and too broken to fight for her pup, she
succumbs to the inevitable, thus committing Max to
what she knows will be a living HELL!

Slowly the massive head lowers. The weary eyes
close and the life she no longer wants ebbs silently
away. Quietly she passes from her last day of life to

. . . .

On **The First Day of Death** she opened her mind for
thought. Sight was now a thing barely remembered.
Eyes that once gave the delight of dimension and
color now lay forever unseeing in the cold shell that
lay beneath the freshly turned earth. Images dance
before her...................................

Made in the USA
Charleston, SC
08 July 2016